NO BACKING DOWN

NO BACKING DOWN

JUSTICE BEGINS™ BOOK FOUR

MICHAEL ANDERLE

LMBPN Publishing
PMB 196, 2540 South Maryland Pkwy
Las Vegas, NV 89109

Version 1.00, January 2022
ebook ISBN: 979-8-88541-056-4
Print ISBN: 979-8-88541-057-1

THE NO BACKING DOWN TEAM

Thanks to the JIT Readers

Dave Hicks
Zacc Pelter
Dorothy Lloyd
Deb Mader
Rachel Beckford
Diane L. Smith
Debi Sateren
Kelly O'Donnell

If I've missed anyone, please let me know!

Editor
The Skyhunter Editing Team

DEDICATION

To Family, Friends and
Those Who Love
to Read.
May We All Enjoy Grace
to Live the Life We Are
Called.

— Michael

CHAPTER ONE

Tyler Katakura, the first Executioner of Atlantica, had originally intended to let the man live. Then he saw something that changed his mind.

The sentry stood near the edge of the densest part of the jungle. He was positioned at an angle so his back was mostly to Ty, although had he been facing him, it's unlikely he would've noticed anything regardless. They were deep into twilight, and the fronds, leaves, and vines of the dense temperate rainforest masked everything in curtains of black. The drifting clouds of white mist reduced visibility still further.

As for the man himself, he was wearing budget, hand-me-down military gear that had probably belonged to Batista's men before the Castro takeover. He held a Chinese surplus SKS rifle and wore a Fairbairn-Sykes combat knife at his side.

He also wore a necklace from which two severed human ears dangled.

Ty's fingers curled around the grip of the wakizashi belted to his side. The ears made the nature of the situation clear. The guard wasn't merely some average schmuck hired to do basic security work, oblivious to the nature of what went on at the secluded hunting lodge. He knew exactly what the owners did. He might've participated in it too.

Long years of practice had taught Ty to contain his rage, to discipline it until the time was right. He waited.

It took about another two minutes for the guard's focus to waver and for him to turn his back completely to the dark patch where the Executioner waited. The day's light was almost completely gone. Somewhere off to the left, a nightbird sang.

Ty sprang into action. Leaping up from the ground, barreling through the foliage, charging the short distance toward the man with the rifle, and drawing his sword was all one fast, fluid motion. The man had enough time to pivot toward the sound but not enough to see what was going on or make the necessary judgments.

The short blade pierced his side, sheared up under his ribs, punctured his right lung and probably his heart, and certainly some of the veins and arteries surrounding the organ. Ty's free hand came up and clamped around the guard's mouth as the man jerked and thrashed in pain. He twisted the blade as he pulled the man to the ground.

Although Ty stopped the body from striking the ground too hard, and his left hand prevented the man from crying out, there was nothing he could do about the rifle. It fell from the guard's grasp and *thudded* onto the turf. Cursing silently, Ty heaved the corpse into the weeds and ferns, secured the rifle, and returned to hiding in the foliage.

If other sentries had heard the commotion, brief and muffled as it was, things could get ugly fast.

Ty sat and waited. A skill he'd developed during his service in the Korean War came in handy now. His mind was free to think, but his animal instincts remained at the peak of alertness. The slightest stimulus would pull him one hundred percent back to the present task at hand, ready to act in less time than it took for his heart to beat.

While nothing happened, the half of his mind that could allow itself to relax turned to the chain of events that had led him here tonight.

After finally locating the missing children he was looking for about four weeks ago, a variety of relatively small jobs had filled his time. Despite the ominous sense among the Executioners that something big was coming—something related, perhaps, to the mysterious Coven of Miracles—Atlantica's usual raucousness, violence, and corruption had seemingly gone into a period of dormancy.

The most recent case assigned to Ty had brought him into the misty jungles that covered the island's interior, beyond and between the hills that ringed Atlantica City to the north. Some of the island's poorer folk, itinerant laborers mostly, had set up a crude but thriving agricultural community in the area. A portion of them worked temporary jobs in the city. Mostly they culti-vated fruit-bearing trees and shrubs, traded with the fisherfolk who lived on the coast, and gathered other minerals or useful plants that they took to the city to sell.

Someone had begun harassing them. At least, that was the language that Eleanor Cervantes, Ty's handler, had used. By "harassing" she meant "murdering."

At first, it had seemed clear what was going on. Now, as had happened many times before, Atlantica's ruthless class of wealthy overlords desired the land where the laborers squatted and sought to forcibly evict them so they could develop it for their purposes. The murders, Ty estimated, were part of a targeted campaign of intimidation to convince the settlers to disperse on their own initiative. That way whatever cabal of rich people behind the shenanigans wouldn't have to go to the trouble of hiring enough thugs to get rid of the entire community in one fell swoop.

Ty had gone into the job grim but confident. Before the formation of the Office of Executioner, he'd worked as a hired gun for a small village in the foothills near the capital. His job was to drive off the goons who periodically showed up to harass the locals and steal the land on which they'd settled.

It didn't take long after he'd arrived in the jungle to realize that what was afoot was something else entirely. Something worse.

As it turned out, a tightly knit cabal of deviant rich people who'd read that old story *The Most Dangerous Game* and decided to take it to heart inhabited the new mountain lodge. Most of the victims were missing trophies from their bodies. Ears, for example. Things that the hunters could take back to prove they'd bagged their quarry, thereby earning greater boasting rights.

The awful truth of the situation had been clear before anyone knew the lodge's location. Through a stroke of luck, Ty had obtained a reliable lead. He'd captured one of the cabalists during a hunting trip of his own. After bringing the man back to the city and applying a variety of highly persuasive interrogation techniques, he'd learned the location of the hunters' secret headquarters.

Now, here he was.

In truth, the lodge was more like a chateau. Its members all seemed to possess vast financial resources, and they'd pooled them to create the most luxurious possible getaway spot to launch their adventures in murder. It lay on a terrace-like ridge on the slope of a massive hill, hidden by the dense trees and undergrowth of the Atlantican forest until one was nearly on top of it. It would've been difficult to spot even from the air.

Ty's conscious mind returned totally to the present and the task at hand as another sentry approached. The man's gait was unhurried, but there was something subtly tense about his movements and demeanor, suggesting he might've suspected that things were amiss.

He was moving in a straight line toward the patch of thick

grass where the first sentry, the man Ty had killed, had been standing.

The Executioner quickly estimated how much time he would have to act if the new sentry saw or smelled blood and looked too closely at the foliage where his unseen nemesis waited. He would be alert, unlike the first man.

Getting to him in time, and taking him out with the sword before he could call out or open fire, wouldn't be easy. Ty might have to shoot him instead and risk alerting the entire household earlier than he would prefer.

The tall, lanky man with a large bushy mustache stopped at the exact spot where his coworker had died. His eyes darted around. Then he kept moving in the direction he'd been going, but at twice the speed. He was heading for the chateau's front entrance, probably to report an irregularity to the head of security or the hunters themselves.

Ty inhaled deeply through his nose. He would have to move fast.

As soon as the man was out of sight, he darted from the jungle, making virtually no sound, and hugged the low wall that ringed the lodge proper. Moving around it toward the corner, he suddenly stopped.

Someone was watching him. He saw nothing, but the feeling, the crawling of skin on the back of his neck, was unmistakable.

He pantomimed doing something with his belt to give himself a second to figure out what was going on. It almost seemed as though...

A twig snapped. Ty swung his head toward the sound, out in the jungle. His well-trained eyes caught the barest glint of moonlight off the glass of a rifle scope.

He jumped sideways, farther than he thought possible, springing to the corner to grab it and swing himself around as the sniper fired. They had a suppressor on the barrel, but that only meant the noise of the round was quieter and didn't echo.

The last thing Ty saw before he pulled himself to momentary safety was the hole the slug made in the wall. It had punched clean through and had to be a .308 at least, perhaps even a .30-06. Not a 50-cal. Nonetheless, whoever was behind the rifle was serious about killing whatever they shot at.

The sniper fired again. Since Ty was out of sight, it was a blind shot, an estimate. He threw himself forward, hit the ground, and rolled over his shoulder as the second bullet tore through the wall about a foot above his head. He came out of the move and regained his feet.

The front entrance to the chateau was only a few yards away. By this point, the two rifle shots had drawn the people's attention inside the building. Voices were raised, wailing in sudden fear or barking orders. Boots tramped on the ground.

Ty sheathed his wakizashi as he moved and unslung the AR-10 rifle he'd carried over his shoulder. The time for subtlety had passed. The only sensible approach was the most brutally direct one.

Which, in all honesty, was the way he preferred it.

As he charged through the ungated entrance in the wall toward the locked heavy doors of the lodge proper, one thing confused him. It had lodged in the back of his mind and stayed there, refusing to keep quiet.

The sniper probably wasn't working for the hunters' cabal. Whoever they were, they were a third party, interested in killing Tyler Katakura but not seeming to give a shit about the people within the chateau.

As Ty barreled toward the doors, someone—seemingly the very guard who'd hurried away a moment ago—popped up from one of the tall windows beside it with a rifle. He never got the chance to fire. Ty's gun found him in a split second, and he popped off two rounds.

The muzzle flared, and the rifle report rang across the clearing. The man's mouth fell open as he staggered back, glass shattering around him. Two dripping crimson holes appeared in his body, one in the center of his chest and another higher and to the side on his right shoulder. He dropped out of sight and never got back up.

Ty swiveled the rifle toward the entrance and fired again, a single shot that blasted out the lock and latch, and the heavy wooden doors swung open. The Executioner was standing on the threshold before they'd finished their arcs.

Within, the lodge was every bit as swanky as it had looked from outside. There was a borderline comical veneer of "ruggedness" to it, with faux log-cabin siding, a grand stone fireplace, and a mounted deer's head to emphasize that it was supposed to be a hunting lodge. Otherwise, it could as easily have been a mansion in the city. The carpet was thick and rich, the curtains worked with cloth-of-gold, and the mahogany furniture topnotch.

Clustered in the center of the sitting room, which Ty saw through an open door past the foyer, were at least half a dozen individuals. The motley band exuded an aura of wealth.

Standing next to the doorway was a man with a gun. Unlike the outside sentries, he was high-end professional security with an armored vest like Ty's and an M-14 rifle. He wore dark sunglasses and a helmet and fell into a shooting stance as Ty raised his weapon. Which man lived and which man died would be a matter of fractions of a second.

However, the first to shoot was someone outside.

The round ripped past Ty, so he heard it whistling beside his ear. It also missed the guard by half an inch, zipping over his arms and under his chin. He flinched and lost his grip on the rifle.

It was all the opportunity Ty needed. He threw himself aside against the foyer wall, flipped the selector switch on his AR-10, and fired a burst in full auto. Two or three of the six or seven rounds took the man in the chest and neck. He squawked and toppled over backward, firing a round into the ceiling. Sheetrock dust rained down on him as he died.

The people in the sitting room—Ty's true, main targets—were all screaming, snarling, and jostling one another. They appeared to be going for weapons.

From out in the jungle beyond the wall, another rifle round popped off. This one streaked through the foyer at nearly a ninety-degree angle from the first direction. Ty's eyes widened. There was more than one shooter. They were pinning down the whole chateau with a crossfire.

He popped the half-spent magazine from his rifle, loaded a fresh one, and charged into the sitting room while bellowing at the top of his lungs. He was alone, and he'd lost the element of surprise. The tactics that remained to him were speed and intimidation.

An older bald man with a bushy white mustache and pointy chin goatee to go with it pulled a shotgun off the wall and fumbled for a pair of shells. Ty flipped his rifle back to semiautomatic and shot the man as he ran, firing three rounds. The first missed, but the second two took him in the chest and stomach. The man let out a barking cry and tumbled over into the fireplace. Fortunately for him, it wasn't lit.

Ty's focus shifted to the other group members—a dark-haired white man and woman, an Arab sheik-type in a traditional robe and keffiyeh headdress, and a fat copper-hued man. His background was impossible to determine at first glance. Ty pegged the remaining olive-skinned woman as probably Cuban, hence the Batista-surplus outfits for the sentries.

All of them were staring straight at him. He raised his rifle, about to shout at them to hit the floor, when the Cuban woman pulled a tiny pistol from her blouse and fired at him.

She missed him by at least a foot, but her trigger finger was fast enough that Ty ducked and rolled all the same. His armor was proof against most handgun rounds, but ironically someone who was a poor shot was perhaps more likely to hit him in the head or limbs—a trained shooter would've fired at his chest.

With the opportunity provided by Ty's evasive maneuver, the sheik rushed over to the guy with the white mustache and grabbed his shotgun. The heavyset coppery man dashed over to a gun rack where several high-powered hunting rifles rested.

The Cuban woman bared her teeth and advanced toward Ty, shrieking at him in Spanish and firing her pistol again and again. It couldn't have held too many rounds, but Ty wasn't about to give her the chance to catch him in the throat with a stray shot. He sprang up from his roll, aimed, and shot her in the face. Her head snapped back, shooting blood straight up, and she slumped to the floor.

As Ty spun toward the Arab, his heart jumped into his throat. The man was faster and more skilled than the Executioner would've guessed and already had the shotgun trained on him.

Then two shots rang out at once. Not both barrels of the coach gun firing simultaneously, but two rifles from somewhere far outside the room. One slug took the sheik in the side above the hip, and the other struck him in the back of the neck. He flopped, gurgled, and fell over.

The shotgun struck the floor, and one of the barrels went off. It blew a hole through an expensive couch, and the man and woman with the dark hair scrambled away, uninterested in fighting.

Ty was wondering if the hidden snipers were on his side when another rifle round struck the floor mere inches from where he'd knelt a moment ago. *No.* They were the foes of everyone else in the building. They wanted Ty *and* the cabal of hunters dead.

He threw himself toward the fireplace, seeking the extra cover provided by its heavy stone sides, and looked at the gun rack where the fat man was bringing up a rifle. The guy fired quicker than Ty would've liked. The round smashed into the fireplace's mantle, and a chunk of stone fell across Ty's face, knocking the rifle from his grasp.

The fat man worked the bolt and fired again. Although he had some skill, in his panic he was point-firing instead of properly aiming down the sights, which cost him accuracy even at a distance of only five or six yards.

Rather than scramble for his rifle, Ty drew his 1911 pistol from its holster at his hip. He aimed at the wide silhouette of the copper-hued man and squeezed off three rounds. The .45 caliber slugs made sharp *cracking* noises as they left the barrel.

The man gasped. Ty found his AR-10 and crept forward, blinking through the cloud of dust from the collapsed mantle. He'd hit the heavy man in the leg and gut, and he'd fallen to the floor, writhing in pain but still trying to bring his rifle up for one last shot.

He never got to take it. Ty shot him twice more in the head, killing him instantly. Then he holstered his pistol and looked around.

Another rifle shot rang out. This time, it must've struck a stud as it punched through the wall since its trajectory altered drastically and it ricocheted across the floor at a crazy angle from where it had originated. Ty ignored it. Still, the fact that at least two active shooters lurked in the forest made everything more complicated.

During the general chaos, the last two residents had managed to hide while everyone else struggled. Now they used an end table to climb out one of the shattered side windows. Ty saw them out of the corner of his eye as the ricochet skidded in front of him.

He turned and sprang toward them. It was dangerous and stupid to do so. There might be another guard hiding somewhere, or one of the pair might have a concealed handgun. Not to mention, he still didn't know exactly where the sniper fire was coming from or how many more hidden rifles remained trained on the lodge.

Capturing or eliminating the "hunters" was his primary objective. He could deal with everything else later.

Ty took a running jump at the small table propped next to the window. He vaulted onto it and hurled himself forward the instant his feet touched the wooden surface, careening through the broken window and over the edges of the glass, toward a thick bush next to the chateau's outer wall.

"Shit," he muttered as the bush's brambles engulfed him. He twisted aside, ripping free of it, thankful for his armor, and sprang back to his feet.

The two escapees hadn't gone for the front gateway through the wall. They'd headed toward the lodge's back yard instead. A large outbuilding lay there, a shed or garage of some sort. Ty sprinted toward them. Nothing suggested that they were armed or about to lay an ambush for him. They were simply trying to get away.

Their actions made Ty think it would be better to capture them alive than to gun them down, although they undoubtedly deserved it. Other people might be involved in this foul operation, and he wanted to know who.

Another rifle shot streaked past him from somewhere out in the jungle. The snipers couldn't see through the chateau's outer wall so they continued to blind-fire based on sound and logical estimates. Unless, of course, one of them had slipped within the wall without Ty's noticing them.

He was faster than the two, but they got into the building before he could catch them. He could've shot them. That wasn't his Plan A.

As Ty kicked in the side door, rifle in his hands, he nearly wasted a precious second as shock overtook him.

The outbuilding wasn't a space lined with tools or even a car. Instead, it housed a hulking, military-grade armored personnel carrier. The two hunters were already scrambling atop it, ready to sink into its metallic interior and make their getaway—or maybe their last stand. Unlike many such vehicles, this one didn't have a machine gun mounted near the hatch.

Ty leapt onto the treads as the latter of the two, the woman, slid through the hatch. His hand shot out, grabbed her narrow wrist, and held it. She screamed. He pulled himself up, braced the hatch open with his foot, and dropped in, ready to fight.

Instead of attacking him, the two sank back. The man had flicked on a rather weak overhead light, and Ty saw them shrinking in terror. They looked similar to one another, with light but tanned skin, long straight noses, dark hair, and pale blue eyes. They were probably brother and sister, or perhaps cousins.

Ty aimed his rifle at them. "If you know how to operate this thing, drive us out of here. Someone is still gunning for all of us. You two might get to keep your lives. Do it." He unsheathed his wakizashi with his left hand and rolled the gun back over his shoulder. Firing a rifle in a small, enclosed, metallic space might render him deaf. The sword could fulfill his threat as easily.

They hesitated. Ty's patience was thin after all he'd been through, but he gave them a second or two to consider it. Then the man lunged at him.

Ty's reflexes responded instantly and without conscious thought. The blade in his hand licked across the man's face, opening a red line along his jaw, the back of his cheek, and part of his lower ear. His hands clawed wildly in the air and Ty slashed him again across the inner thigh, a few inches above the knee. He collapsed, groaning and bleeding.

The woman reached out and took him by the shoulders, allowing him to fall back into her arms before resting him against the console.

Ty pointed his sword at her throat. "You have two options. Either you can die, along with him—he's your brother, isn't he?—or you can fire this thing up and get us out of here. Take us back to Atlantica Metro and my associate, Dr. Costa, can get him patched up, stop the bleeding, cure any infections...maybe even fix his face a little. You need to hurry. We have to leave *now*. What do you say?"

She shot him a hateful glare but turned and started the vehicle. Ty allowed himself a tiny bit of relaxation;. He remained alert and maintained his grip on the wakizashi but felt confident that his two new friends would cooperate.

Not only would he be able to shake them down for information later, but their little toy would get him safely out of the woods. On foot, with at least one talented marksman after him, his chances of getting home alive would be far slimmer.

The APC growled and chugged as the woman piloted it out of the shed, then through the rear opening in the chateau's enclosing wall. There was a faint trail through the jungle that led down the mountain's western slope. The problem, Ty recalled, was that there was nothing in that direction save a jumble of hills and a deep ravine.

Gunshots continued to ring out. Two impacted the vehicle itself but merely *dinged* off the thick armor. Ty hoped that his hidden adversaries didn't have anything explosive. Their rifles might've overcome normal building materials but would be useless against heavy steel plating.

During the war, Ty had been in APCs a couple of times, but he'd never driven one himself. He was a grunt. His experience lay in crouching in the mud and dealing with the enemy in an up-close and personal fashion. Good thing the woman knew how to drive.

It was a rough ride. The APC bumbled over the irregular terrain, sometimes drifting alarmingly on steeper ground, although its powerful treads were enough to overcome most obstacles. Ty helped the man get some scraps of cloth onto his cuts to staunch the worst of the bleeding.

"What's your name?" he asked.

The man refused to look at him. "Hugh," he muttered.

Ty nodded, then looked at the girl. "And you?"

"Tilda." She, too, didn't look at him, but she was absorbed in managing the vehicle and watching the periscope.

Ty nodded. "I'm Executioner Katakura. You might've heard of me. I don't fuck around. I also keep my word. Your activities will receive a fair evaluation when we return to the city. That's all I can promise you. Hugh, you'll get medical care. Justice will be served, one way or another."

They rumbled on in silence. Ty glanced at the screen and saw, with a sudden jolt of alarm, that Tilda was driving them straight toward a cliff. They'd passed over the western hills and were right on top of the ravine.

"Hey," he said. "Turn around. Head south."

Tilda sighed and ignored him. The edge of the cliff, and the dark void beyond, loomed closer.

Ty cursed himself for making that stupid comment about justice. His two captives knew the reputation of the Executioners —there were reasons why the organization had been so-named. The brother and sister had little hope of a sentence other than death unless they could prove that they had no involvement in the lodge's human-hunting endeavors.

The Executioner raised his sword and let the tip touch the woman's shoulder so a flick of his wrist would split open her neck. "Don't do it," he ordered her. "You might get a plea bargain, a reduced sentence if you cooperate and help us with the investigation."

His words had no effect, and with horrifying desperation, Tilda pushed on a lever that *increased* the APC's speed. Before he could react, their front end sailed over the cliff's edge.

Ty swallowed and froze. Since the action now doomed all three of them, it was pointless to kill Tilda. As his gut felt like it sailed out of his body and vertigo seized hold of him, she flipped a switch on the dash.

The fall never came. It was as though they were sliding down a muddy ramp, although the treads were no longer grinding away. Instead, something within the machine hummed loudly. Ty looked again at the screen and saw space receding before them. They were drifting gently toward the ground.

"What in the goddamn *hell?*" He took a step closer to the woman.

Tilda made a low sound in her throat. "Relax, Executioner." The bitterness was thick in her tone. "I will be oh so *happy* to get you safely back to the city. You and my brother."

Hugh had sunk within himself and barely seemed to have noticed the fact that they'd taken a multi-ton military vehicle over the edge of a ravine and were now hovering downward as though the APC were a paper plate.

Then, when they were perhaps ten or twelve feet from the ground on the far side of the gorge, a burst of static and gout of smoke came from the dash. The strange humming gave way to a louder wheezing sound, then ceased altogether.

Tilda exclaimed something, but the sound drowned her out as the APC crashed the last few feet to the ground under the normal power of gravity. The impact knocked everyone around. Tilda fell against the side, Hugh rolled across the floor yelping in pain, and Ty hopped from foot to foot while he braced himself against the latter, his teeth rattling.

When he looked up, Tilda flicked off the switch she'd flipped as they'd driven over the cliff. The smoke and crackling static died.

The acrid smell of burned wires lingered within the compartment, but the APC stabilized itself. Tilda drove them through the rest of the wilderness, soon coming to one of the roads that led into the hills and heading toward the gleaming lights of the city.

Ty inhaled. "Nice trick," he mumbled. He helped Hugh back into a sitting position and reapplied the wad of stained cloth. The leg wound had reopened during the crash.

Then the Executioner waited. Once more he receded into the state of half-focused relaxation where the portion of his mind he could spare for the moment rested while his perceptions and reflexes remained at full alertness.

There was no guarantee that his prisoners wouldn't try something as soon as they thought they could. It was Tyler's responsibility to see them back to HQ.

Even if everything went smoothly on that front, there remained the *other* problem, the burning questions which had no answers yet to soothe them.

Who had been trying to shoot him from the jungle around the chateau? Would they trail him back to base?

CHAPTER TWO

Ty perked up. The less-essential half of his mind had rested, but now he needed its services again. Tilda had brought the damaged armored personnel carrier deep into Atlantica City, and they were no more than a block or so from the Executioners' new headquarters.

If the pair intended to overpower him and escape, he suspected they would do it within the next five minutes.

"Turn right here," he instructed the woman, pointing toward the road up ahead at the next intersection. "It's the second building on the left. Unmarked, with a gate out front."

Tilda nodded. She still refused to look at him, but at least she was cooperative for the time being.

The APC's treads were tearing up the asphalt. Ty felt bad for whoever would end up having to repair it, but at least they would be paid for their services. Atlantica had no government to speak of and technically no laws. Private enterprise or mutual agreement provided everything.

That was how the order of the Executioners had come into being. Tyler Katakura had been the first, agreeing to the position after a classy Mexican lady, Eleanor Cervantes, had approached him about it and proven that she and her backers were reliable.

That group called themselves the Executives. They were the more conscientious of the island's wealthiest citizens. They'd funded the creation of a new pseudo police force to rein in the rampant crime, violence, and corruption that had plagued Atlantica from the beginning.

From consisting solely of Ty and any random allies he could scrounge up at first, the order had expanded to four members. It still wasn't much. Given the quality of equipment, training, and experience each Executioner had, Ty felt it was a damn good start.

The APC rolled to a stop in front of the gate. Ty had no intention of getting out to open it himself. Instead, he climbed the ladder, pulled out his pistol, and held it on Tilda as he opened the hatch and popped his head out.

A figure came out of the building and saw him. Nodding, they approached the gate, unlocked it, and swung it open. Looking down, Ty saw that it was the third Executioner, Dr. Gaje Gurung. His friends called him Gage.

Ty glanced down at Tilda. "Bring it in. Pull up along the side of the building, over that way, then stop and turn off the engine. I'll get our doctor out here ASAP, and we'll get your brother taken care of."

Hugh responded with a low, breathy groan. Tilda said nothing but did as Ty instructed. He continued to cling to the ladder. A sharp braking motion might've jostled him loose, but all it would take was a single gunshot within the compartment to cause havoc that she might not be able to avoid. For now, she behaved herself.

Once the APC stopped, Ty helped Hugh up and out, with the man's sister supporting him from below on the ladder, and they carefully got him out and laid him on the ground. Tilda stood over him while Ty, confident that the two weren't going to flee or do anything else stupid, went over to greet Dr. Gurung, who'd followed them over.

"Hi, Gage," he began. "I have a wounded man here, so get Dante. He's not out on a mission, is he?"

Gage was a short, slightly rotund, balding, and bespectacled Nepali man, a former Gurkha who'd since become an archaeologist. Then an Executioner. People tended to grossly underestimate him at first sight since he was *usually* a polite and genial man.

He nodded. "Yes, Dante is here. I will get him immediately. Do you need help with anything else?"

"In fact," Ty added, glancing back at the massive military vehicle, "we're going to need some repairs on this APC. I figured you could handle that. Might as well grab Daria while we're at it since I can debrief you all while we're dealing with the mess."

Gage smiled. "Of course. I will be back." He turned and moved away at a trot.

Ty wondered if it might be easier for them to have support staff who coordinated stuff like this. The Executives could probably afford it, but it would create certain complications since hiring people who were both competent and trustworthy was always difficult.

Particularly on Atlantica, where everyone and everything was for sale.

While the older, smaller man went to fetch their friends, Ty watched over his captives. The siblings seemed like normal humans at the moment. Vulnerable, and they clearly cared for one another. It was almost enough to make an observer forget the revulsion that came with knowing why the Executioners went after them to begin with.

Ty's eyes wandered over to the building. It had originally been a private gymnasium, and the first floor reflected that, with the four of them using it as a training center. There were also apartments on the second story, where the Executioners now lived. At least some of the time.

It was a definite improvement, Ty thought. In the earlier days, each member had to provide their lodgings. They had no real headquarters, preferring to meet instead in a suite of rooms at a hotel that Daria had reliably used before she joined.

The arrangement had worked out well enough, particularly since Daria had an actual house that wasn't too far from the hotel, unlike the rest of them. Ty's only home to speak of was a shack in the small village he'd protected before the Executioners formed.

Gage had lacked any particular nest, also. Dante had effectively been living on borrowed time when he and Gage had gone up against a Soviet hit squad a few weeks ago. He'd had nowhere at all to go when they'd recruited him.

So they'd decided that everyone should stay together in one place.

The Executives, acting through Ms. Cervantes, had come through and secured the usage of the current locale. Ty wanted to make it more defensible, with a ditch and barbed wire and lots of alarms. For the time being, a fence and a gate would have to suffice.

The real issue wasn't so much attacks on the building, Ty felt, but attacks on their vehicles—the so-called Autocutioners, the fleet of heavily armored trucks that ferried them around on their various errands and misadventures.

Ty had directed Tilda to park the APC near the Autocutioners. A lot adjacent to the building was partially protected from the elements by an awning and a partial wall. The open section could be covered with a tarp without too much difficulty if an especially nasty rainstorm blew in.

They sometimes had other vehicles present, working on them or improving them, so it was helpful to keep out excessive moisture. That was a nearly impossible task on Atlantica at times since the climate tended to be humid and drizzly. Tonight the weather was clear.

A couple of minutes later, the side door to the structure opened, and out strode the other three Executioners. Despite being the one who'd taken charge of summoning the remaining two, Gage trailed in the rear. Dante Costa, the tallest and youngest of them, was out in front, and Daria Barruk was in the middle.

Dante gave Ty a quick, respectful nod before rushing to Hugh's side. He'd brought a medical bag with him and opened it as he knelt beside the man, pulling out dressing for his wounds, antiseptic, and a few other implements. He went to work without speaking, examining the slashes on the half-conscious man while the woman stood over them both, glowering.

Gage headed toward the APC to examine it. Cars and trucks weren't his specialties, but he had enough mechanical and technological knowledge that he could usually get them pointed in the right direction when it came to vehicular repairs.

Daria slowed her pace and stopped beside Ty. She was a few years older than him, closing in on forty, but still spry and attractive. A Polish Jew who'd escaped from the Nazis as a young woman, she'd spent some years in America before coming to Atlantica as a smuggler. Or, by the time Ty met her, a semi-retired "smuggling consultant."

"Oh." She glanced at Hugh and Tilda. "They're alive. May I ask why?"

Her tone was of legitimate curiosity. She had no authority that superseded Ty's and wouldn't have been able to chastise him even if she'd been sarcastic.

Ty grunted. "Reasons. Help me get the woman handcuffed and stashed somewhere secure. She's playing along for now, for the sake of her brother, I think, but I'm not stupid enough to trust her for long."

Daria laughed. "Of course. You might lack a certain amount of subtlety, Mr. Katakura, but I never regarded you as 'stupid' in the slightest."

"Thanks." He strolled toward the pair with Daria in tow. Even after knowing one another for months, she still called him "Mr. Katakura" most of the time. It didn't bother him. His American side might've preferred to be called by his first name, but his Japanese side was more than comfortable with formality.

Once Tilda realized that Ty and Daria were walking straight toward her, she tensed. "What's the matter? I've done what you asked. What are you doing?"

Ty smiled at her. "Yeah, and thanks for that. I don't feel like keeping an eye on you every second, so we're going to put you in cuffs and let you have a seat in my truck for a little while."

She made a few scoffing sounds and briefly looked like she might resist. Wisely, she didn't. Daria watched her while Ty retrieved the restraints from his Autocutioner, then he opened the back of the truck and had her sit on the bench. She pouted at the floor as he shut the doors on her and locked them.

"That ought to make things simpler," he commented. "Anyway, we're making a legitimate effort to save her brother."

From where Hugh lay, Dante piped up, "Yeah, yeah. He's not in much danger of actual death, but did you *have* to cut him right along the jawbone *and* into his goddamn ear? This shit isn't easy, you know."

Ty strolled past Dante and patted his shoulder. "I do know. That's why we rely upon you to do it."

Leaving the Italian-American physician to his work, Ty and Daria headed back toward the building. While Ty waited next to the entrance, Daria went in for another first-aid kit and came back out to examine Ty's wounds.

"I'm not badly hurt." Various aches and stings were becoming more noticeable with every minute his body relaxed after the rush of combat. Still, he had no reason to believe he'd taken any serious injuries.

She flicked a hand. "Badly, no, but let me look all the same. You might have picked up an infection out in the woods like that. Ah, you're all scratched up. Did you jump into a bush?"

He sighed. "Yes."

"Why on Earth would you do that? I imagine you had your reasons. Here." She poured some alcohol onto a piece of clean gauze. "This will hurt, of course."

Ty stood, his face grittily stoic as Daria wiped his various minor abrasions. The sting was severe. It was strange, he thought, that the pain of healing a minor wound could be tougher to bear than the pain of taking the original injury in the heat of battle.

When the process was close to complete, Daria repeated her question from earlier. "Why are they still alive? You were authorized to wipe them all out."

"Truth be told," he grumbled, "I wasn't sure I could operate that APC myself. I was an infantry grunt. Mechanical stuff was never my strongest suit."

Daria nodded. "Yes, I see. Why the hurry?"

Instead of answering her directly, he added, "Also, I felt they should stand trial in front of the people they were terrorizing. I offered them a plea deal of sorts. That will be up to the farmers. Who will probably hang the fuckers. At least the two of them will get a last meal or two and a night's sleep first. In the meantime, they got me back here in a timely fashion."

Daria frowned, the way she did when her mind was turning over a particularly messy problem made of a tangled mass of ethical concerns, practical difficulties, and other obscure notions that only a smuggler might've thought of.

"I'm concerned that we might need to find a better way of dealing with people like this," she declared. "We cannot keep doing it this way forever. To simply drop bodies where we find them is sloppy and uncivilized. It creates unnecessary terror and the impression of brutality."

Ty didn't entirely see the problem with that, but he valued Daria's opinion enough that he chose to withhold judgment until she'd spoken the entirety of her piece.

She went on, "Turning the guilty over to local communities to enact bloody vengeance themselves only deepens the divisions that run through this island, the tribalism, and the 'every man for himself' attitude that prevails outside the tribes. It's not the way forward in the longer term. It will cause us problems as time moves on and the Executioners grow in number."

Ty glanced at the other two members of their still-minuscule organization. "What do you mean, Daria? Too many bodies piling up in too short a time, something like that?"

"That, yes, but not only that. It also could create division among *us*. Do you see? We cannot reverse a verdict of execution. We can challenge it after the fact, but it would do no good." She crossed her arms over her chest—probably trying not to reach for another cigarette—and her eyes grew distant.

It took a second for the full implication of her words to sink in. "Oh." Ty's tone betrayed his slight but growing aggravation. "You're saying that we can't necessarily trust the judgment of our fellow Executioners. Someone might kill some people, only for another one of us to say, 'Hey, you had no right to do that, you prick.' Something like that."

She responded with two slow nods.

Ty's jaw clenched, teeth grinding, and his fingers curled into fists merely thinking of the prospect. The ability to operate unfettered, and to have absolute confidence in the loyalty of his comrades, were two of the most important things that made the job bearable and worthwhile.

"Are you saying that you don't trust the rest of us to make good decisions?" He tried to keep his tone neutral, but Daria was subtle enough that she probably picked up on his slow-burning anger regardless.

She fidgeted in place. "I trust the three of you. But all of us, who are members so far, have been vetted by the others. We know one another well, have fought together, and trust one another. Still, our group must grow. As we bring in new Executioners, some conflicts and disagreements will be inevitable."

She glanced past Ty, toward where Gage and Dante worked side by side. The two of them had become friends weeks before Dante had joined the Executioners. There was no question that the two of them trusted and relied upon one another.

Daria looked back at Tyler, the man who'd recruited her.

"When there are ten of us, or twenty, or fifty, will the moral code of each be the same? Will we all be able to evaluate the judgment of them all, and will the actions of every member be one hundred percent agreed upon by every other? As we grow, Atlantica, too, will become bigger. More people come here on the ferry every day.

"How will we avoid a situation where there are different camps of Executioners, who have different factions of the populace as their supporters and allies? What if an Executioner who is popular in the west but hated in the east kills someone from the east and must answer to that region's Executioner of choice? It could be a recipe for disaster."

Ty scowled. He didn't like what he was hearing. But...

"You have a point," he admitted. "That's many years in the future, isn't it? We have other things to focus on in the meantime."

Daria rolled her shoulders. "Yes, true. Is there anything in particular you had in mind? Besides the obvious." She flicked her eyes toward the APC.

Ty breathed in deeply. "Yeah. Yes, there is. When I was at the hunting lodge, it wasn't only them and me. Someone else was there too."

His fellow Executioner arched an eyebrow. "Oh?"

"At least two snipers, hiding out in the surrounding jungle. Maybe more." He narrowed his eyes, thinking back to the sinister gleam of moonlight on the first rifle's scope. "It was hard to be certain, but I think they were trying to kill me *and* my targets. They weren't working with the hunters, and I sure as hell didn't ask them to be there. We have a third party involved. Someone who wanted all of us dead."

Daria's face stretched as the blood drained from it, and her jaw went slack. Ty was grateful for the reprieve. He'd planned to report on the mysterious shooters all along. His fellow Executioners deserved to know and might be able to help him unravel the enigma they represented.

By changing the subject, he also bought himself an extra moment or two to ponder Daria's gloomy predictions. The thought of the Executioners becoming too big to manage themselves, overripe with corruption and factionalism, making Atlantica worse rather than better... It wasn't a pleasant notion to consider.

Daria abruptly made a sputtering sound. "Why did you not tell me sooner? Why did you not announce it to all of us at once? This is important! If someone is hunting *us,* we have a greater problem on our hands than only these scum." She flourished her hand toward Hugh and Tilda.

Ty smirked. "Well, you didn't ask. Better late than never though, right? Besides, they were on foot. They wouldn't be able to trail us back here yet, especially since we jumped a fucking gorge with that APC. That's another thing we need to discuss."

Daria threw up her hands. "We must have a meeting. All four of us. We must discuss this in privacy." She lowered her arms and stared, squinting into his face. "Did you say *jumped a gorge?*"

CHAPTER THREE

"Well," Dante quipped, taking off his latex gloves and depositing them in the trash receptacle, "getting him the hell off the pavement outside and into a bed was a step in the right direction. Which reminds me, if I'm going to be doing proper doctor stuff here, we need a gurney. It's an essential piece of equipment."

The four of them stood outside the room where they'd locked up the two murderous siblings. Hugh lay sedated on one of the beds while Tilda sat beside him in a chair. Ty had removed the handcuffs. They no longer seemed necessary as long as she was confined somewhere without the possibility of escape.

Daria rolled her shoulders. "Yes, yes. You have a radio like the rest of us. Call Ms. Cervantes and tell her. If the Executives can outfit us all with armor and weapons of our choice, to say nothing of state-of-the-art vehicles with Atlanticore engines, I'm certain they can provide a single gurney."

Dante interlocked his fingers and flexed his hands, cracking his knuckles. "Let's make it two, in fact. Never know when you might need an extra one."

Ty asked, "Okay, so how's he recovering? Stupid thing to ask since they'll probably face execution in another day or two. Still, I gave my word that I'd get him treatment before they stood trial."

Paying no heed to the latter portion of what Ty had said, Dante reported, "He'll be fine. He lost more blood than I'd thought, which is why he was so weak and kept passing out. Aside from the blood loss and the possibility of infection, the wounds weren't going to be fatal no matter what. I gather that was the idea. If you wanted him dead, he would be."

Ty responded with a single slow nod.

Gage took a step forward. "I've learned a most useful thing or two about the APC," he proclaimed, his Nepali accent fading. "It might perhaps be better to discuss this other matter first. Of the people who were shooting at Mr. Katakura."

He had long been relatively fluent in English, but he'd noticed his grasp of the language gradually improving the more time he spent in the company of his friends. Of course, the British English he'd learned as a young man was noticeably different from Tyler's or Dante's American English or Daria's secondhand continental European English.

"Yes," Ty agreed. "I could use a cup of strong tea. Or coffee if it's all we have. Then I'll tell you the rest of it. It potentially concerns us all."

The room where they'd imprisoned the two "hunters" was originally little more than an oversized closet, but Dante had converted it into a simple, makeshift recovery room. It lay on the second floor, in the center of the building, with no access to windows or other avenues of escape. So it made a good impromptu jail cell, as well.

The quartet descended to the rec room on the first floor, which doubled as their sitting room and communal dining area. Gage made tea for Ty, Daria, and himself, while Dante dispensed the last of the day's coffee from a machine into a paper cup. Although not exactly hostile to tea, he was too thoroughly American to prefer it when the other great caffeinated beverage was available.

Ty arranged his chair to face the other three. "All right. I already told Daria the gist of it, and she might've mentioned some to the rest of you, so forgive any redundancies."

Dante waved it off. "Yeah, yeah, you're forgiven." For a second, he looked sheepish and tensed as though he'd done something wrong and expected punishment. Then he relaxed.

Ty glared at him, though only for half a second or so. He first encountered Dante over two months ago while fighting a ring of gun smugglers. The gang had co-opted the young physician to act as their medic, and only a couple of lucky breaks had saved him from being blown away or cut down with the rest of them. Ty had kept Dante on probation, insisting that he heal Gage's broken ankle. Eventually, the Gurkha had prevailed on the others to admit Dante into their order.

Ty cleared his throat. "Someone is gunning for me, and maybe not *only* me. When I got to the chateau, I took out one of the sentries. As I was about to attack the place, I saw a rifle scope out in the forest. They tried to shoot me and damn near succeeded."

He summarized the rest of the battle, fielding the expected questions from his partners about whether or not the unknown snipers might've been working in conjunction with the hunter cult.

"I doubt it," Ty opined. "They probably could've afforded high-level marksmen to watch over the place, but if by some chance they were the ones who hired these people—and there had to have been a minimum of two—they must've skimped on cost and got what they paid for. The snipers were putting bullets through the house, over and over again, with no concern for the hunters. I think they were trying to kill *everyone*. Me and the inhabitants both. They took out one bastard, some Arab oil prince, before he could shoot me. Then they tried to add me to their notch count. Good thing they failed."

Daria stroked her chin. "You are certain they weren't confused as to who they were shooting at? Or that it wasn't simply random suppressing fire? They couldn't have seen everything going on within the house."

Ty shook his head. "No, I'm not *certain* of anything. It didn't feel like that. I've been under sniper fire before. The two shooters, or possibly more, were arranged at different angles. They couldn't always see us, but the whole thing seemed to me like a concerted effort at systematically annihilating everyone on the hill."

"That is most disturbing," Gage murmured, his bushy graying brows bunching over his eyes.

Dante snapped his fingers. "Could be there's a contract out on all of us. As in, maybe you were their main target, and they figured they'd wipe out all the bastards at the lodge while they were at it to leave no witnesses. Make it look like the hunters or their guards fatally wounded you right before you finished the last of them off."

Daria glanced at him, then back at Ty. "That could be. What do you think, Mr. Katakura?"

"Not sure. None of you have been attacked, have you? I'm the only one so far, " he pointed out.

Everyone else shook their heads. Then Gage's eyes widened.

"The rest of us were all here, together." He glanced at each of them in turn. "Tyler was the only one who was alone. This made him an easier target. Perhaps, then, it would be wise for us to stay together until we know who these people are and what they're doing."

Daria nodded. "I agree. It might be that the snipers were there on behalf of a personal vendetta against Tyler, specifically. If their target is the Executioners in general, they will find it far more difficult to kill all of us at once."

"So, no more solo gigs for a while," Dante surmised. "Maybe that's just as well. I get bored working alone. Which reminds me, we ought to get ourselves a nurse. Ideally one who's, you know, under thirty and stacked." He held his hands out in a cupping gesture in front of his chest.

Daria snapped, "Charming, Dr. Costa. Let us contact Eleanor and see what she has to say. Her sources may provide some information as to who these assassins might be."

Ty smiled grimly. "Her sources are usually good. What I wonder, though, is how the snipers knew I would be on that mountain at that time. If they had that intel—or if they were that good at tracking me even when I was making an effort to remain unseen—they probably know where I'm heading next."

Gage squinted. "Ah, where is that? I am afraid I don't recall."

"The farming valley next to that same mountain," Ty explained. "The community those two, and their sick friends, were terrorizing. I have a promise to keep. Handing our friends Hugh and Tilda over to them is the last part of the mission."

Daria snapped her fingers. "*You* are not going there, then. We are. We will take two trucks, with two of us in each, and the prisoners separate as well. That will make things hard for them, should they try to ambush us."

Dante leaned back in his chair and folded his hands behind his back. "Yeah, sounds good. I don't have anything better to do. We're talking about tomorrow, right?"

"Yes," Ty confirmed. "Provided nothing else comes up first."

Gage's pleasant, fatherly face was morose, as though something troubled him. After a long sip of tea, he finally voiced his lingering concern.

"Tyler. You said you gave these people, Hugh and Tilda, a 'plea bargain,' yes? That they would stand trial? If you turn them over to the farming community, they will kill these two. Should you not keep your word?"

Ty grimaced. "I am keeping my word. The farmers will be the ones to conduct the trial. Yes, they'll probably sentence them to death. Like I said, this way at least they'll get a last meal or two before the end comes and time to mentally prepare for it. Plus, I will be enforcing that dictate we put out a few weeks back—the one about cruel and unusual punishment."

Daria had once again folded her arms in front of her. She used to smoke clove cigarettes frequently but was trying to cut back. Smoking too much made her get out of breath quickly, and she wasn't getting any younger.

"Good," she said. "Local communities must enforce justice themselves. Still, to allow horrible methods would benefit no one. If someone must die, it should be clean. I will support you in ensuring the farmers understand this, Mr. Katakura."

Dante muttered, "The sons of bitches probably deserve worse than a 'clean' death, but yeah, you're right. Burning them at the stake would only scare people and maybe create misplaced sympathy. Feels strange saying as much when I patched up the one guy, but both of them are probably best dealt with by a swift rope or a bullet to the head."

Gage's expression had softened slightly, but he still looked uncertain. "So be it. Perhaps the farmers will agree to a sentence other than death." His tone suggested that he doubted it, but saying it aloud seemed to make him feel better.

It was odd, Ty thought, that Gage was such a good-natured individual when he could be so ferocious in combat when he had to. The aging Gurkha still carried his heavy kukri knife and had split open men's heads with it on multiple occasions. Some of those occasions had been *recent.*

During the Second World War, if Ty recalled correctly, Gage had driven a goddamn fuel truck into a Japanese plane. Dante had made an offhand comment about how the small Nepali became a completely different person in battle.

Ty's ruminations abruptly ceased when Dante spoke up. "Speaking of last meals for the twins there, we need to stock up on provisions again anyway. I'll get up early and handle it." He looked down at the cup of coffee in his hand and frowned. "Dammit."

Daria snickered. "You're still young. You will manage. I have a bottle of Polish vodka that will make you unconscious in no time if you have trouble getting to sleep."

"Noted," Dante quipped. "What would we do without you, Daria?"

Before she could attempt to reply to the rhetorical question, Ty reclaimed control of the conversation. "Before we settle in for the night—Gage, I'd like you to brief me on what you found with that APC. Daria, Dante, it might not be a bad idea to join us. If not, we'll tell you tomorrow."

Daria had risen and was fishing around in a cupboard for the promised bottle of vodka. "If he can explain it here, then yes, we should all listen. Gage, can you tell us about it without needing to *show* what you mean?"

Gage stood. "Yes, I believe so, but if you want more detail, we must look at the vehicle in person. I can explain most of it."

Dante smirked. "We believe in you, bud. Go on."

Everyone else shut up as Gage regaled them with his findings. While Dante had tended to Hugh and Daria to Ty, he'd examined the damaged armored personnel carrier and tried to unravel the mystery of its hovering ability.

Ty had suspicions about how Tilda had made such an enormously heavy vehicle float like a hang glider. Now, it seemed, those suspicions were about to be confirmed.

"The APC has—or rather, if you will excuse me, *had*—a most complex harness of rare metals that are unique to this island, wiring in strange configurations, and Atlanticore crystals." Gage held out his hands as he spoke. He seemed to be unconsciously pantomiming the operation of a small machine. "This very likely explains how it could levitate in such a fashion."

Daria snapped her fingers again. "Yes, yes. When I first met you at the archaeological excavation site, you demonstrated how

Atlanticore could cause certain metals to rise in the air. I do not understand how it works, but I have seen it."

Gage nodded. "Indeed. Sadly, we were unable to learn how it worked before our team disbanded. It seems that this APC operated on a similar form of technology. However, it burned itself out. It was probably not well-tested and intended to be used only as an emergency measure."

Ty remarked, "It served its purpose, then."

"Of course," Gage affirmed. "Although you are most fortunate. Atlanticore can be volatile, and the system they were using appeared very unstable. I am surprised it didn't explode and destroy the vehicle."

Ty thought back to the night he and Daria had overtaken a barge sailing out from the island, trying to stop it before it got too far out to sea. Smugglers had put a massive load of the strange blue crystal below deck, and for reasons unknown, Atlanticore exploded if taken too far from its source. He'd also used a small charge of the stuff to blow up a hostile smaller boat while he was at it.

"Yeah," he muttered. "I've always been lucky. What I want to know, though, is this. Would it be possible that this cult, this group of people-hunters, could've created a setup like that on their own? Or did someone else gift it to them, or show them how to do it?"

Dante and Daria watched and listened. Daria had poured vodka for both of them, but they remained focused on the discussion.

Gage shrugged. "Anything is possible, perhaps? From what I can tell, the APC's crystal system is similar to devices we've seen used by the Coven of Miracles. Even the soldering patterns are much alike. My engineering background wasn't primarily in automobiles, I must say. Still, there are characteristics that many different kinds of machines can share. So I believe a single person is designing and constructing these crystal power matrices, or at least a group of people who have all learned the same techniques."

Dante commented, "Makes sense. There's a quote or something—I forget who said it—about how a given school or institution will always stamp its mark on all its students. The people who learned to do something from the same master will share the master's quirks. Something like that."

He threw back a hefty gulp of vodka and gasped as the crisp burn of its high alcohol content set his mouth afire, trying not to cough.

Daria looked faintly amused as she sipped her helping. "We should ask our guests what they might know about such things. The woman was familiar with the device's operation although she might know nothing about its construction."

Ty stood. He was the last of the four to rise to his feet. "Agreed. But not tonight. It's getting late, and I doubt they would be much help at this hour. Not to mention, we're getting tired too." He thought about adding something about how Daria and Dante were getting drunk, as well, but decided against it. If it became a problem, he could raise it later.

"In the morning, then?" Daria surmised.

Ty shook his head. "We'll have to question them while we're on the road. I don't want to delay. The farmers from the valley they were preying upon were already restless when I climbed that mountain. I have a promise to keep. Dante, go ahead and get them a nice final breakfast. But come the morning, we're not wasting any time."

Dante agreed, but Gage seemed a tad confused about the hurry. Rather than explain the intricacies of Atlantican politics that underlay the whole situation, Ty opted to focus on the logistical details of their operation tomorrow.

"As Daria suggested," Ty began, "we'll split up. Gage and I will take one Autocutioner with Tilda. Dante and Daria can take another and handle Hugh. Different routes. We'll coordinate our departure times to arrive at about the same time, and keep in touch over the radio. Be alert for threats."

The other three all stared at him. Daria was the first to say what they were thinking. "You mean, the snipers."

Ty nodded. "Them, or anyone else. Those two might have friends who could try to rescue them at the last minute. Whoever we might come up against, don't underestimate them. Honestly, I barely made it out of the lodge alive. If they'd had more mercenaries guarding the place, or if I hadn't seen the scope at the last instant, or if Tilda didn't happen to have an armored vehicle out in the shed, I might not be here now."

Dante took another swig of vodka, smaller this time. "Point taken. Especially since everyone says you're the scariest one of us."

"Thanks," Ty grunted.

CHAPTER FOUR

Hugh and Tilda Ashcroft requested, for their breakfast, a surprisingly simple repast of scrambled eggs, coffee, and Danish pastries. Dante picked up the Danishes while he and Daria shopped for food in general. Ty handled the eggs and coffee. He made enough for all six of them.

Once Dante returned and the food was ready, Ty made platters for the two captives and took them into their room on a tray, telling them to enjoy it but be ready to depart in half an hour.

"Oh, we certainly will," Tilda quipped in a cold tone. She avoided making eye contact, but not out of fear. It was more to slight him.

Hugh let out a snorting chuckle. Although still in a certain amount of pain from his injuries, he was noticeably better, and the sedatives Dante had given him had worn off overnight.

Ty ignored their response and left, locking the door behind him. They would probably need to use the restroom before departure, and he'd scheduled for that along with everything else.

He wondered why he bothered or cared. Twenty-four hours ago, he was ready to gun them down like rabid dogs. Twelve hours from now, both would probably be reposing in a shallow grave at the jungle's edge.

As he walked back to the station's rec room to enjoy his breakfast, it occurred to him. *Civilization.*

Atlantica, lawless though it was, was trying to become civilized and desperately needed at least a veneer of the niceties, formalities, and courtesies of a true society. Although he'd been born and raised in America, Ty nevertheless had grown up with the residual politeness and respect for tradition that reigned in his family's native country. Japan, despite its mass psychosis during the war, was a place where even the rituals of death were subject to rules of decorum.

In truth, so were most other societies. The barbarism whereby blood spilled and the bodies cast aside, forgotten as soon as they were no longer *useful* to anyone, was a horror unique to war zones, where order, let alone courtesy, had broken down and ceased to have any meaning. Despite the grim activities suggested by their name, the Executioners weren't there to act as a band of organized murderers. They were the hands of justice.

Thus, the loathsome pair locked in the infirmary would have their last meal, their courteous treatment, per Tyler's bargain with them. Then they would be delivered unto justice, per the Executioners' obligations to the burgeoning attempt at civilization on Atlantica.

Gage had gone out to the garage area to check on the two vehicles they would be using. Daria and Dante were already lounging in the dining area of the rec room.

Ty sat between them after pouring himself a cup of black coffee. He glanced at both in turn.

"Daria. You look as though all you drank last night was water." He bit his tongue to keep from laughing too soon. It would be better to maintain a straight face for as long as possible.

She waved a half-eaten Danish vaguely in the air. "Of course. I had only a single glass. Of vodka, I mean, not water."

Ty broke down snickering.

Dante looked at both with red, squinty eyes. "Ha, ha. I get it. Well, Katakura, I'm surprised you *let* me drink since you always struck me as the type of hardass who would have forbidden it right before an important operation like this."

"I probably should have," Ty mused. "I might've overestimated your tolerance."

Dante chugged coffee. "I'm fine, mostly. I drank a glass of water before bed, and some nutrition and caffeine will take care of the rest. Anyway, you paired me up with Daria, and her liver seems to be a marvel of human biology. Daria, is that a Jewish thing or an Eastern European thing?"

She shrugged. "Both, perhaps? We drank sacramental wine as children and moved on to vodka as adolescents."

"Well," Dante shot back, "Italian kids drank wine too. So it must be the vodka. That crap is serious."

Ty forked eggs into his mouth. He took a certain satisfaction in noticing that they had been cooked exactly right, neither too runny nor too dry. "All joking aside, let's go over the plan again.

"If we do this right, and with a bit of luck, it will consist of nothing more than taking a drive out into the country to drop off a package and heading back home. Only one or two things going wrong can be enough to turn it into a nightmare. I want everyone on top of their game. No bullshit, no mistakes."

His partners agreed. He knew Daria and Gage would appreciate the situation. Dante was the only one who potentially worried him. Even then, his doubts about the young physician were minimal. The four of them were increasingly proving to be a highly effective team, a well-oiled machine.

Soon, they were all out in the parking lot and ready to go—all six of them.

Hugh and Tilda both wore handcuffs with their arms secured

behind their backs. Each pair of Executioners lifted one of the siblings into the rear of their respective vehicles before shutting and locking the door.

Dante glanced up at his charge. "He'll be fine," he said of Hugh. "Still, I can see why you wanted me in the same truck as him. In case my amazing medical skills become necessary, that sort of thing. If you'd put the woman in with him, though, my dashing good looks would've—"

"I'll drive," Daria cut him off. "You watch the prisoner and handle the shotgun. Try not to talk too much, please. Outside of the interrogation."

Ty and Gage wished them well. The route they would be taking was the slightly longer of the two, so the plan called for them to depart a couple of minutes earlier. Daria nodded goodbye as she piloted the Autocutioner out of the lot, past the gate, and into the city.

Gage offered to drive. "It is good to get more practice. I'm surprised by how quickly I've picked it all up again. I did not drive trucks of this size for many years."

"Yes, good." While Tyler didn't doubt Gage's skill with a gun, he doubted his own even less. He climbed into the passenger's side.

As Gage fired up the Autocutioner, Ty reflected that the Executives had finally standardized the fleet. At first, they had given him a great behemoth of an armored truck before giving Daria one that was little more than a glorified pickup.

Gage's—the one they now occupied—had been about halfway between the two, and they'd all agreed that it was the ideal size for most situations. Nimbler and easier to hide than Ty's massive older one, but stronger and with more storage space than Daria's. Plus it helped when members of an organization used similar or identical equipment. It made it easier to pick up the controls if one of them became incapacitated.

That led Ty's thoughts to the subject of weapons, and he

briefly wondered if they'd made an error. Gage and himself both carried AR-10 rifles. Daria preferred an Uzi 9mm submachine gun, however, and Dante an Ithaca 12-gauge shotgun. Good enough firearms for *most* situations, but pistol rounds and buckshot were of little use against anyone in heavy armor.

"Dammit," he muttered. "We're going to have to assign a rifle to each Autocutioner. Whether they use it as their primary weapon or not, they should at least *have* one if they need it."

Gage glanced at him. "I am sorry, what did you say? I have my rifle."

Ty shook his head. "Yeah, I know. I should've given one to Daria and Dante. I'll have to trust that they can handle themselves regardless."

As the Nepali pulled out of the lot, he stopped so Ty could hop down and close the gate behind them. Then they resumed their journey, making for the road that led due north into the agricultural zone in the foothills, immediately below the mountain where the hunters' cabal had sequestered themselves.

Ty glanced at the back compartment. Tilda half-lay along the bench within it, staring at the floor. To Gage, he said, "Keep an eye out for anything suspicious and remember to check in on the radio at the agreed-upon intervals. I'm going to go ask the lady a few questions."

He climbed past his seat and opened the door, sitting on the opposite bench. The ride was smooth enough so far on the paved streets of Atlantica Metro, but would get far bumpier once they reached the dirt roads that wended through the hills.

"Tilda," he began. "I'd like you to answer a few questions."

The woman looked up. She was rather attractive, but simply knowing who she was robbed her of much of her appeal. The bitter, haughty look on her face didn't help, either. "Oh? Questions about what?"

A vague sinking feeling in his gut told Ty that the conversation probably wouldn't be productive. Tilda had recovered enough from yesterday's events to take on an air of defiant mockery. She most likely grasped that their former victims would execute her and her brother in a matter of hours, which couldn't have done much to make her feel cooperative.

Of course, if she didn't talk, there was still the prospect of Eleanor Cervantes coming through with useful intel. Ty had called her earlier that morning and told her everything, requesting that she radio them back as soon as she had something worth reporting.

Ty pushed such concerns from his mind and held Tilda's gaze, his expression stern and serious but otherwise neutral.

"About the APC that you drove away from the lodge. I'd like to know where you got it from, how it was able to hover through the air after you drove off that cliff, and who made that possible. If you legitimately aren't aware of any of *that*, I want to know who were the contacts and providers that your... group...worked with."

He paused, giving her a second to think about it, then added, "You can't take back what you and your brother have done, Tilda. However, you can do something good, for once. Help me. Help me so I can put an end to all the wrongdoing that's been going on."

Tilda stared at him with a blood-curdling mixture of disgust and boredom. "Why would I want to *take back* anything I've done? It was *fun*. So much more interesting than your life must be, acting like a dog for your benefactors, waiting to be patted on the head. The people we hunted were dull, stupid individuals, not much more than animals anyway. They had nothing to look forward to but farming, farming, and more farming. We did them a favor, I should think. They got a thrill, and we relieved them of the burdens of their useless little peasant lives."

Ty sat in total silence. He couldn't tell if this was truly how she felt or simply an act to annoy him, a posture she was adopting to mock her captors.

If she *didn't* truly feel that she was justified in hunting down random human beings like wild hogs, it raised the question of why she'd joined the cabal to begin with.

A tremor of barely suppressed rage went through the Executioner's body. When he spoke again, his voice was softer but colder.

"I will pretend you didn't say that if you drop the stupid fucking act and stop trying to behave as though you'll have the last laugh. You won't. Salvage something from your miserable existence now by giving me information I can use to help people, or forever hold your peace."

The woman laughed in a deliberately nasty way, her periwinkle-colored eyes flashing.

"I'm at peace already. Whenever I feel the slightest bit unhappy, I think back to the family of four Hugh and I took a month ago. He let me take the first shot. The father's head came apart like an overripe cantaloupe. Then Hugh shot the mother in the back. It only took us another ten minutes to run down the children. They couldn't move very fast, after all."

Ty only resisted the urge to drive his sword through her throat because mingled with his anger and horror was a profound confusion. *Why,* he wondered, would she boast of something like that? Why would someone be so utterly unapologetic for acts that the whole world recognized as evil?

"So," he began, "you enjoyed murdering men, women, and children. Who supplied the rifles and the bullets? Who pointed you toward that particular family? Who covered for you when the inquiries started? If you want to brag about something, brag about that."

Tilda laughed again. "You are incredibly crude and unsubtle, Executioner Katakura. You should break kneecaps for the Sicilians instead of wasting your time pretending to be a cop. You failed to find us in time, anyway."

Ty's left arm shot out and grabbed her roughly by the hair,

while his right hand smacked her across the face hard enough to send her tumbling back to the end of the bench. He was on his feet, advancing, unable to think of anything except destroying his target.

The woman's mouth distorted in a jeer of defiant fury, and there was a trace of fear in her eyes—but not as much as there should've been. Not enough for what Ty was about to do to her.

"Tyler!" Gage called, sharp and impossible to ignore as his voice came through the open doorway. "Come back up here, please."

Ty's head swung toward the front of the truck, his eyes still blazing with black fire. "Stay the fuck out of this, Gage."

Gage cleared his throat. "Eleanor is on the radio. Come, please talk to her. She says she has information for us."

Ty inhaled through his nose and let the breath out through his mouth. He closed his eyes and counted to five. When he opened them, Tilda was looking back at him.

"I will be back to finish this conversation later," he promised her.

Then he pulled himself forward and around the seating block, kicking the door shut behind him and lowering himself into the seat. He angled the radio toward his face to better hear Ms. Cervantes. He took the microphone from its hook.

"Hi, Eleanor, it's Ty. What do you have for us? Over."

The woman's voice, with its faint Guadalajara accent, replied, "Hello, Mr. Katakura. I've researched the issues you raised and heard back from several of my contacts. We suspect that the people you describe might be independent contractors. Please allow me to explain the general situation before I move on to specifics. Over."

Tyler frowned. Mercenaries. That was more or less what he'd expected, but it still could potentially be bad news. "Yeah, we have time to listen. Go ahead. Over."

"A few different groups that are operating on Atlantica defy easy classification and don't seem to possess any particular loyalties. They haven't resolved themselves into more standard security operations. They work at the edge of normal life and are rarely seen or spoken of. Such groups usually will take contracts from people who are very high in society. The nature of their work will reflect this."

Pausing in silence, Ty wondered what the hell she meant by that. The main thrust was easy enough to understand, but he sensed that Eleanor was speaking in deliberate vagaries and expecting him to read between the lines.

He asked her to clarify. If she did, so much the better. If she didn't, that too was useful since it meant Eleanor might be trying to warn them that they'd stumbled onto something they weren't supposed to know about.

What she said next wasn't a clear case of either. She kept talking, providing more information, but without stating anything too bluntly.

"These outfits are typically the best such people available. Lesser groups, who lack the skill, experience, or toughness, tend to have poor chances when they confront real security forces who are well-funded and well-trained.

"If they take dirty jobs from criminals and commit things that would be serious crimes in most places instead, their actions would attract the attention of the Executioners. No one wants that. In a way, the quality of independent contractors on Atlantica has grown greater and more dangerous as a direct result of your many successes. Only the most fearsome will take on high-profile jobs, lest they cross your path. Over."

Ty managed a grim smile. "I suppose that makes sense. I know the type of people you're talking about. Do you have evidence that they're high-end mercenaries, or is it simply conjecture? Is there anything to suggest that they might be a hit squad working for an actual government? Over."

He nearly regretted asking the latter question. If foreign

agents were again trying to subvert things, it raised a vast host of complicated legal and ethical concerns.

Notably, no nation would ever admit to sponsoring such a squad because it would violate the rest of the world's universal policy regarding the island—TINA, or "There Is No Atlantica." The politicians found it too difficult to agree on how to deal with the emergence of the planet's newest country. Instead, they'd all officially defaulted to pretending it didn't exist.

Eleanor made a low humming sound. "Hmm. No, it's doubtful, I think. There are too many consequences involved in violating TINA. Scrutiny of such matters has increased since Gurung and Costa exposed the recent efforts of the Communist countries to subvert our affairs."

Gage raised his eyebrows at that. It must not have occurred to him that the price of success, sometimes, was that one's enemies became craftier and more cautious.

Ms. Cervantes continued. "I tell you all of this as general background information. We do have relatively reliable intel on who these people may be. My contacts obtained useful hints. We suspect that they're an outfit called the Ghost-Makers, a small group who are, how do you say, tight-knit. And, it seems, tight-lipped."

She paused, and Ty committed the slight rudeness of interrupting her. "Makes sense. Mercenary companies usually value discretion. I haven't heard of them, though. How many of them are there? Who's their leader? Where have they fought before? Over."

"Their numbers are unknown but assumed to be small. They behave like a wolf pack, working with little oversight and hiring their marksman-caliber rifles to expensive and reliable employers. A woman who seems to be something of an urban legend leads them. Her ferocious and ruthless reputation sounds much like yours, Executioner Katakura.

"Rumor has it that they've served in South Africa, Vietnam,

Ireland, and Algeria. I would be almost certain it was them, but there's one complication. Over."

Ty exchanged a glance with Gage, who'd been listening in while he drove. The Gurkha shrugged, and Ty turned back to the radio. "Yes, what complication? Over."

"The Ghost-Makers tend to refuse jobs that are dirty or excessively complicated. I should think that taking out a hit on an Executioner would qualify as 'dirty,' and perhaps 'complicated' as well."

At that, Eleanor abruptly stopped speaking, as though she'd meant to say more, only to cut herself off at the last instant. Ty waited for a second, and she spoke again.

"Do be careful. The word is that the Ghost-Maker outfit has never failed to fulfill a contract. As such, they might see it as a point of professional pride to finish you off. Of course, this might make them more vicious in their methods, and therefore more reckless. Perhaps frustration will help draw them out. Over."

Ty ran a hand through his lank black hair, which grew shaggy once again. He tended to forget to have it cut until it became impossible to ignore.

"I see. Yeah. Any clues about where they work out of? Here on the island, I mean. Over."

Eleanor shuffled a paper or two before she responded. "Only gossip. It appears that the mystique of the unknown gives them great satisfaction. People have suggested everything from a holdout in the jungle to a lair in the sewers beneath Atlantica Metro. So far, there's nothing solid."

Ty nodded. "All right. Thank you, Eleanor. If you have nothing else to add, then out."

"Good luck, Executioners. Out." Static crackled and her voice faded away.

Ty looked back through the window into the rear compartment. Tilda was looking at them with a lazy mixture of interest and loathing. She'd been trying to listen in but might not have heard much through the heavy door.

She would be irrelevant by nightfall, though. Ty turned his face back to his partner. The old soldier who'd since become a scientist would have far more valuable things to offer than the wealthy woman could.

"What do you think, Gage?" His tone was low, gentle by his standards but impregnated with a healthy dose of professional worry. They might soon find themselves facing a truly formidable adversary.

While keeping his eyes on the road, Gage began, "I'm concerned about the situation. Eleanor seemed to have only rumors and hearsay. It's better than nothing, but we cannot assume the truth of anything she said. If even *some* of it is true, and if what you described to us from last night is also true, then to be frank, I'm surprised that you are still alive."

Ty blinked. He hadn't expected to hear that. "Oh? Do you know something I don't?"

"One skilled gunman," Gage elaborated, "who is going after a single target who is unaware, should not be too difficult, yes? Of course, there is the paranoia that we all must have from working as Executioners to consider. But they sent an entire team after you. Or part of one; you say there must have been at least two, perhaps more. I wonder what went wrong..."

Ty relaxed a bit and let out a low, snorting laugh. "Well, they were pretty good, but one of them crunched a stick underfoot. It happens to the best of us. The moon reflected some light off the one's scope glass. If it hadn't been for that stroke of luck, they might've taken my head off."

Gage sighed. "That is not what I'm talking about. The point of multiple sharpshooters is redundancy. You see? If the first cannot kill you, the second should. If not them, surely the third. I wonder—how many levels of failure occurred within a most professional and motivated team of snipers? And, how many of those failures were *intentional?*"

Gloomy silence set in as neither man spoke. The older Gurkha waited for a response while the younger *nisei* digested what he'd said.

Ty tried not to squirm. For one thing, it implied that Gage didn't think Ty had been able to escape the shooters under the auspices of his skill. He disliked his fellow Executioner underestimating him.

However, Gage might have a point, and that notion was still more unpleasant. Simply having assassins out to kill him, bad as it was, had the advantage of simplicity. It was easy to understand. It meant that all he had to do was keep an eye out for them, not die, and repel or destroy them before they could complete their mission.

If the snipers had knowingly and willingly *allowed* him to escape with his life, it bespoke an agenda beyond his comprehension. It meant that the situation the Executives had sent him into wasn't something he could shoot his way out of.

Gage broke the silence with a request. "May I try to speak to Ms. Tilda once we arrive? I might, perhaps, achieve some success by trying a different method. We should have a short time after we arrive before the farmers come to get her."

Ty waved and glowered out the window at the buildings. Smaller and sparser, now; they were passing through the city's outskirts and would soon enter the hilly countryside beyond.

"Yeah, sure," he agreed. He tried not to think too hard about Tilda's sneering boastfulness and deliberate efforts to piss him off. "Although I doubt it will do much good."

CHAPTER FIVE

It was probably just as well that Ty had returned to the front passenger seat and stayed there after Eleanor had called. Once they got out of the city, there was a jumble of hills to drive through, and the Autocutioner clanked and jostled as it ground over the rutted dirt tracks. They drove through gullies and over ridges, and branches and leaves from the surrounding jungle reached out for them. The hefty vehicle smacked them all aside without inconvenience.

Still, Tilda must've been uncomfortable with only a hard bench to sit on. He couldn't say he felt particularly sorry for her.

As time wore on, it occurred to Ty that his timing might've been off. The route that Daria and Dante were taking was technically longer in terms of raw mileage. Still, it was an easier drive. They were detouring around the steepest part of the foothills and entering the valley closer to the coast.

By contrast, the northern route that Ty and Gage had chosen was more direct. Yet it was impossible to drive through such a rugged wilderness at the same speed one could go on relatively flatter and better-maintained roads down on the plain. As such, he worried that Daria might arrive well before he did. Then he would have to listen to her complain about it.

He shook his head to clear out the unworthy thoughts. Any difference in their times of arrival couldn't be too massive. Daria probably wouldn't care *that* much. The dispiriting experience of trying to interrogate Tilda had poisoned his mood.

At last, Gage squinted and pointed ahead of them, the tip of his finger brushing the windshield. "There."

The hills had begun to level out a few minutes ago. Atlantica's strange temperate rainforest had originally overgrown most of the valley beyond them. The last several years of human development had pushed the jungle back, transforming the area into more of a savanna dotted with thickets and tilled fields.

A mile or two farther ahead was the village. Gage's attention and Ty's focused on something closer. The crossroads where their route intersected with the longer, less direct one. Another Autocutioner was parked there.

"Damn," Ty muttered.

Gage brought the truck closer, braking to a halt perhaps ten yards from Daria's vehicle and slightly off the side of the road. The ground here was flat enough to provide enough room to do so. In the higher elevations they'd passed through, there wasn't space to swerve to avoid another motorist if it had been necessary.

Ty opened the door. "Wait here a moment. I'm going to talk to Daria before we do anything else." He hopped down.

Ms. Barruk descended from the driver's seat of her Autocutioner almost the same instant she saw Ty. Rather than meeting halfway, Ty allowed her to come to him. It was safer that way, keeping her closer in case any hazards waited for them deeper in the valley.

"Hi," Tyler began. "How long were you waiting?"

She put one hand on her hip and flapped the other. "Oh, perhaps three minutes. An acceptable difference, I would say."

Ty nodded, trying not to let his relief seem too blatant. "Good. I forgot how rough the terrain on our route was. Any problems?"

When Daria replied in the negative, Ty mentioned that Gage wanted to attempt a further interrogation of Tilda. Daria had no objections, especially since she and Dante had no luck to speak of in getting any information out of Hugh. The man had given them a couple of vague, useless answers and pretended to zone out from the painkillers.

Dante's voice called from the truck, "Which is bullshit. The dose I gave him wasn't that strong. I should have given him pain-*revivers*. If those existed."

Ty ignored the quip, but he was impressed that Dante could hear them so well from thirty feet away while still in the vehicle. He looked past the other truck, toward the little town and the various agricultural homesteads surrounding it. It appeared that a crowd was forming near the south edge of the community—coming to greet them, no doubt.

Daria stepped closer. "Tyler. When Gage has done his questioning, let me be the one to hand the Ashcrofts over to these people. There's no reason for you to expose yourself to unnecessary danger since the assassins might've embedded among them."

Ty protested, "What? What about everyone being a target? I thought we agreed that they were probably after all of us. You'd be in as much danger as I would."

She held up a finger and retorted, "That was only a guess. We *know* they're after you and can only estimate or assume that they *might* be coming for the rest of us as well. A certainty versus a probability. So, sit down and shut up." She finished with one of her playful little smiles to show no hard feelings.

He scowled. "Sit where? Besides, I'd rather be on my feet if they're going to ambush me."

By now, Gage had climbed down from the Autocutioner as well and strolled over to join them. "Tyler, you should appreciate that Daria is willing to go into the line of fire to protect you.

There is no need to despise courage when it serves the well-being of others, even if it involves telling you to shut up. Ha, ha..."

Ty's temper flared up, but he forced himself to keep it under wraps. His friends were doing the right thing. Or trying to, anyway.

Daria walked off toward the distant crowd. She'd left her Uzi in the vehicle but still had her pistol in its holster on her hip. Just enough persuasion in case the group became hostile, but not enough to deal with serious threats.

Ty reflected on the woman's original choice of sidearm—a Walther P38. The irony was perverse. She had ditched it a couple of months ago, though, for a Browning Hi-Power, which was an objectively better gun. Although Ty failed to understand what Europeans saw in 9mm.

He sighed and turned to Gage. "Yeah, she's probably right. Plus her people skills are exceptional. Compared to mine, anyway. She's really the heart of the group."

"Indeed," the Nepali agreed. "It is good to have her binding us together."

The moment of warmth was interrupted by a sudden gagging sound from within the truck. "Good Lord," Tilda shouted. "How sickening. How long have you two been sleeping together? I mean you and the woman, of course. Or do I? Perhaps all of you together at once. Your pillow talk must be *awful*, though."

Ty's eye twitched. He turned away from Gage. "Excuse me. I'm going to go break her jaw."

"Wait." Gage clamped a hand on his shoulder with surprising strength, holding him in place. "Please. You promised me earlier that I could talk to her. We might still be able to get information. Breaking her jaw will do nothing to help anyone."

His nostrils flared with mounting frustration, but Ty knew that, again, his friends were right. "Yeah. Fine. Do your thing. If she tries anything, though, I'm beating it out of her." Normally he didn't like hurting women, but in some instances, he'd make exceptions.

Ty sat on the stump of a thick old tree that the farmers had cut down some time ago. It was mostly overgrown with moss, and new flowers were sprouting around its base and roots. He waited, watched, and listened.

Gage opened the back of the Autocutioner and beckoned for Tilda to sit on the edge. She did, crossing her legs to sit in a more dignified fashion, despite her hands still being cuffed behind her and the disheveled state of her hair and clothes after the long, bumpy ride.

"Tilda," Gage began, his voice and demeanor gentle, almost grandfatherly. "We have some time. Please, if you do not mind. I am curious. You are a lovely young woman. Why do you behave this way? What has happened to you to make you come to Atlantica and do this?"

Ty looked at his boots. What his partner was doing was probably a waste of time. It might work—Gage's approach of being kindly, seeming curious and empathetic rather than judgmental. Ty suspected that Tilda was too far gone for the older man's efforts to have any real effect.

Tilda snorted. "What has happened to me? My brother and I were bored, and we happened to have the money to come here and find ways to amuse ourselves. That is all. Only the simple and stupid require complex answers for things. Shouldn't you be tilling a field or fetching water for someone?"

Ty muttered, "Yup. Exactly what I suspected." Breaking her jaw might not have helped them gather intel, but it would've spared them all having to listen to the woman's filth for so much as a moment longer.

Still, Gage persisted. His patience and mercy were, by Ty's standards, apparently unlimited. He cajoled her for three or four minutes, ignoring her snooty and vicious comments until at last, she began to soften. Ty had no idea how he did it.

He simply hoped that Daria was all right—although Dante kept an eye on her from their truck—and that the farming community's leaders would hurry up with the negotiations and take the Ashcroft twins off their hands once and for all.

As Tilda began, finally, to tell Gage the sort of thing he truly wanted to uncover, Ty's curiosity grew. It quickly proved to be a *morbid* curiosity, though. What the young woman had to say wasn't pleasant to hear.

"Fine," she said. "You wish to know my life's story so you can nod and say something like, 'Ohh, *that* explains it, how clever I am for drawing the connection.' So be it; I'll tell you." A crooked smile spread across the lower half of her face.

Her eyes, however, darkened with sadness.

Gage nodded and waited.

"Our father was a wealthy tycoon back in Baltimore. He held interests in oil, construction, fishing, and other dull and unglamorous industries. To relieve the tedium of managing such things, he took a sexual interest in both me and in Hugh. It made his work so much easier."

Ty felt his gorge rising. Part of him wanted to shuffle off immediately since he had no conscious desire to hear about such things. Yet, he *had* been wondering what could make a person go so wrong.

Gage gave a sympathetic frown. "I am sorry to hear that."

As though he hadn't spoken, Tilda continued, "When Hugh was old enough, Father also encouraged him to rape me as well. I suppose he wanted his son to learn the ropes at an early age. I suppose he wanted me to begin enjoying the company of men. Well, I did. I continued to enjoy his company until quite recently, in fact."

Ty put a hand over his eyes and hung his head. "God..."

Tilda continued her account, explaining how she and her brother bonded emotionally over the shared experience of being abused and manipulated in such a way. Then, one day when they were in their mid-teens, they hatched and carried out a plan to murder their parents. Their mother knew what their father had been doing yet had never acted to stop it. There wasn't much investigation into the "car accident" that claimed the elder Ashcrofts.

Thus, Tilda and Hugh, barely past childhood, became the heirs to a vast fortune. They'd passed the years indulging their whims in any way they pleased. They maintained their incestuous relationship with one another, in addition to taking other lovers on the side, and pursued even worse forms of amusement for as long as they thought they could get away with them.

Finally, about a year ago, their excesses began to draw attention. They decided it was time to leave Baltimore, and indeed the United States in general, lest they be exposed and become international fugitives.

It was during their search for a new home that the Coven of Miracles had reached out.

"They offered us sanctuary," Tilda stated matter-of-factly. "Atlantica, they said, could be our new playground with new toys. We leapt at the opportunity, naturally. Why would we not? It sounded...fun."

Ty looked up and saw the pained, miserable look on the woman's face. He tensed in surprise. After all the other crap he'd heard from her so far, he wouldn't have expected her to be capable of such emotions.

Tilda began to weep, leaning over and sobbing every few seconds. "It still hasn't made me *happy*. Any of it! Or Hugh. Poor Hugh. We only wanted to..." Her voice trailed off.

Gage's lip was trembling as though he were about to start crying as well. Ty hoped he didn't. If Tilda's bizarre story were true, even he had to admit it was, to put it mildly, sobering.

Then she stopped. As suddenly as the tears had begun, they ended. Tilda recovered, staring at Gage with sharp eyes. Her teeth came out in a carnivorous sort of grin, and she burst out laughing, falling back onto the truck's bed.

"Ha! You believed that. I should've been an actress. No—a comedienne. Look at this fool!" She gestured at Gage with her foot. "He's just like the old man. Ha! I bet he gets conned out of his pocket money every time he walks the streets. The whores with their sob stories win him over every time!"

Gage said nothing. Ty couldn't see his face since he was attempting to study the wood grain in one of the roots below him to hide his disgust.

Tilda sat partway back up. "You know, I wish Father *had* the spine to fool around with me. Or Hugh." She gyrated her hips suggestively in Gage's direction, with a half-moaning sigh, exaggerating the perversity as much as she could.

"Then it wouldn't have been such a mess trying to cover up his murder. Who knows, then we might not have had to kill the old woman, too. Self-defense; justifiable homicide performed under abusive duress as the lawyers would say. If only we'd been clever enough to think of that when we were little. We could've been heroes! Imagine the fun we could've had with that kind of reputation, to wrap around ourselves like a pretty new skin."

Ty looked up, watching Gage. He refused to look at Tilda. Secretly, he admitted that he hoped the ever-sanguine older man would lose his temper. Gage was pleasant all the time, dropping the friendly demeanor only when there was extreme danger to deal with. Seeing him "snap," particularly on a creature like Tilda, would've been oddly satisfying.

He didn't. He only nodded, then motioned for Tilda to get her legs clear while he closed the back door and locked it again. Then he came toward Ty.

Ty inquired, "So how did it go? Sounded like it was a splendid little chat." He'd overheard everything, but he wanted to hear the Gurkha's assessment.

"Oh, it went well, thank you. She lied a great deal to amuse herself. Some of it might've been true. It was difficult to separate the truths and falsehoods, but it would seem her life was full of grave mistakes no matter what. She did confirm something most important, although I don't think she meant to."

Ty raised his eyebrows. "Yeah?"

"The Coven." His friend extended a hand. "They were the ones who sponsored them and gave them their tools. As we suspected. At no point did we use that name around her, so the fact that she used it herself, without prodding, means it was probably not a lie."

Tyler sighed. Being a warrior by nature, he was, if anything, the *least* skilled of the four of them at being a cop. The importance of Tilda's offhand remark had gone over his head. He was grateful for partners whose talent at the subtler sorts of investigations counterbalanced his propensity for simply finding out where the bad guys were and shooting them.

"Probably not," he agreed. "That makes me think, though, that I might have missed something up at the chateau. I had to leave in a hurry."

Gage nodded. "Yes, yes. As soon as this matter is taken care of, we should go there and search for more evidence."

A glance to the side revealed that Daria and the crowd of farmers were approaching. They'd crossed most of the valley and would be within speaking distance in another minute or two. Since Daria was fine, it seemed safe to assume that the Ghost-Makers were nowhere nearby and that she'd negotiated with the community without incident.

Ty looked at Gage. "Well, from what we know of the Coven of Miracles, they're the fastidious types. They seem to think of everything, account for everything, and always cover their tracks. So if this little hunting club was in contact with them, the Coven's people might've already been back to the chateau to clean up. In which case, we'd find nothing." His skin itched with the need for action. They ought to be hurrying up to the lodge right now.

Gage, marvelously enough, remained calm. "That is possible, yes. We should not waste time. Still, hurrying will not matter if they've thought of that. There is only so much we can do."

The approaching group of locals had stopped about five yards from Daria's Autocutioner, waiting. Dante climbed down from the passenger's seat, presumably to open up the back and get Hugh free for extraction. Daria advanced toward them, waving for them to come over.

Ty stood. His smile was grim. "Looks like it's time for us to offload our garbage." He was looking forward to it. It meant that the day wouldn't prove to be a *total* loss, after all.

CHAPTER SIX

Ty waved at Daria, but she held up the flat of her hand toward him and shook her head. Then she repeated her motion from a moment ago—waving Gage and Dante over. She wanted Ty to stay behind.

"Oh, right," he murmured. "I'm supposedly in more danger than everyone else is. That might even be true." The idea rankled him, but he remained where he was, keeping an eye on things from afar.

It was easier to make peace with it than he would've guessed. In a tense situation like the one his friends were about to wade into, having a man in the rear, ideally on overwatch with a nice powerful long-range rifle, was always a good idea.

He moved toward Gage's Autocutioner at a casual pace, as though he were absentmindedly ambling in that direction for no reason. Once no one was paying attention to him, he would slip into the vehicle and insert himself into the front, directly below the ceiling hatch, which he could use to pop up and take aim if he had to.

Gage helped Tilda down from the back of the truck. She cooperated and slid to the edge. The small man put one arm under her knees and the other around her back to lift her the short distance to the ground. She remained handcuffed. Ty guessed that the woman had spent all her defiant energy on her little spiel a couple of minutes ago and had resigned herself to her well-deserved fate.

At the same time, Dante was drawing Hugh out from the back of the other Autocutioner. The man complied, much like his sister. Ty got the impression that Hugh was recovering from the pain of his injuries and the stupefying effects of Dante's medications. There was a little spring in his step.

The two Executioners and their prisoners marched forth to meet Daria, who said something to them in a low voice before turning. Then they all took ten or twelve steps toward the massed leaders of the farming community.

The farmers, being old-fashioned sorts, had chosen mostly older men to represent them, well-established village patriarch types. There was a smattering of mature women, though, as well as a few men who couldn't have been more than thirty.

Virtually all of them appeared to be armed. Mostly with crude melee weapons—farming implements or other tools such as axes, machetes, scythes, or sickles, and fittingly enough, pitchforks. Ty suspected that one man toward the front had a pistol in his waistband under his shirt, however. There was also one man with a double-barreled shotgun and another with an old lever-action rifle.

Given the mob's size, Ty only hoped that the negotiations didn't turn sour. Despite being poorly equipped compared to the Executioners, there were around forty of them. Enough to do serious damage if they wanted to.

Tyler reached the rear Autocutioner as the discussion began in earnest. The vehicle was at such an angle that he could climb in through the still-opened back compartment and go through the internal door to the front, right below the hatch. He reached up and opened it, leaving it sitting slightly ajar and braced on its heavy latch so more of the crowd's sounds would be audible.

Still, he couldn't hear everything they said. He thought of those wire transmitter things that the cops used when setting up stings on bad guys and wondered if the Executives might be able to requisition some for the team. They could be useful.

He also watched the slopes and trees around them. If the mysterious assassins knew they were here...if they planned to strike...now would be a perfect time.

Through the front windshield, Ty watched the negotiations growing more animated. Gage and Dante stood guard beside Hugh and Tilda while Daria continued to act as spokeswoman. Everyone's voices grew louder, and Ty made out some of the discussion.

It seemed that Daria was reminding the farmers that they had to carry out their verdict within certain standards. The Executioners had agreed that there would be no torture, no cruel and unusual means of death, in incidents of community justice. Only "standard" methods of execution were permissible.

While a few of the elders argued that the Ashcrofts deserved worse than that—which they probably did—the majority of them had accepted Daria's ultimatum and instead were debating over how to do it.

Some wanted to hang the pair from the nearest large horizontal branch, and it looked as though a couple of men had brought generous lengths of thick rope to get the job done. Others preferred to carry out beheadings with the tools they had with them and a nice solid tree stump. There was also disagreement about whether to do it right here or to drag the siblings back to their makeshift town square and deal with them there.

Ty hoped they did it out here, on the edge of the wilderness. His gut roiled at the thought of the local children being around to see people put to death, even people like Hugh and Tilda.

"Here," asserted an old man with a deep, authoritative voice.

"Let's do the dirty deed here and have it out of the way, so we can all get on with our lives."

Someone else, a woman, shouted, "They threatened all of us. They even targeted the *children!* So all of us should see what happens to them now!"

The response was five or six other voices speaking at once, trying to yell over one another, making it impossible to discern individual words or phrases. Ty grimaced. He hoped Daria knew what she was doing. She had, after all, single-handedly managed not one but two opposing angry crowds during her mission at the archaeological dig and emerged mostly unscathed.

Perhaps as a sign of good faith or some such thing, Daria stepped back and unlocked the cuffs that trapped both of the Ashcroft siblings' hands behind their backs. She glared at them before turning her attention back to the crowd.

Then the skin on the back of Ty's neck bunched up, tingled, and tried to crawl off his body. He *knew.*

Someone was watching him.

Ty knew some people possessed from birth a kind of extra sense, an ability bordering on the supernatural. It allowed them to perceive when they were being focused upon, especially by people or animals with malevolent intent. Others didn't have this ability inborn but developed it over time, cultivated it through experience.

Ty didn't know which of the two possibilities applied to him. He'd never really noticed the phenomenon until his service in the Korean War, seemingly so long ago. Perhaps he'd learned it through combat, or maybe he'd always possessed it, and it had simply lain dormant until he needed it.

The one thing he knew for sure was that he *did* have it. Perhaps once or twice out of many, many incidents had he been proven wrong. This moment was unlikely to be one of them.

He moved his eyes before he moved his head to the right. Toward a big, tall, bushy tree that spread its roots in the tiny crevasse between two lumpy slopes, the last of the foothills before the valley proper began and the forest started to recede. Part of the tree didn't look right. There was a mass of...something, a bulk of shadows that didn't belong with the rest, though it was well camouflaged and might have escaped the attention of most people. People who had never had a gun's sights—or scope—trained on their heads.

In one swift, fluid motion, Ty sprang up and popped his upper body through the hatch, knocking aside the lid and trying to bring his gun arm up through the narrow opening. Simultaneously, he turned his head, looking full-on at the offending tree.

All doubt was gone. Someone *was* crouching there amid the branches and leaves.

He angled his face forward again, keeping his eyes on the tree as he shouted at the top of his lungs, *"Hey! Sniper!"* With his left hand, he gestured emphatically at the edge of the woods while his right arm brought his rifle up and out into the open.

Dimly, he was aware of roistering activity in front of him and slightly to the left as his comrades fell into half-crouched battle stances and sought cover, while the mob of farmers began shouting and jostling each other as they looked around.

Most of Ty's attention focused on the tree. The world itself narrowed to only the space that separated himself from the blob of shadows within the branches, the shape that didn't belong there. Two branches rustled and bobbed.

Before his rifle was up and ready, one of the branches transformed as if by dark illusionary magic into the barrel of a gun pointed straight at him.

It was over, then. Amid the strange slowing-down of time that almost always occurred at the commencement of deadly conflict, Ty had room in his head for only a single thought. Death, at last, had found him.

A terrible *crack* split the air asunder, the storm-like report that could only be a high-powered rifle fired from nearby.

The location of the sound was all wrong. No flare leapt from the muzzle of the sniper in the tree. No chunk of lead propelled at supersonic velocity cut through Ty's face, neck, or chest.

The flash came from somewhere else. Ty couldn't say where. What he saw were bits of metal, chunks and splinters of wood, and droplets of blood expanding through the air in all directions from the tree.

The sniper, seemingly a woman by the body shape, plummeted from her perch. She wore a full ghillie suit, covered in brown and green camo plus leaves, fronds, and moss. Blood soaked through her camouflage from her upper body. Ty couldn't tell where the bullet had hit, but it was probably somewhere vital.

She struck the ground in front of the tree, about halfway between Ty and the crowd beyond Daria's Autocutioner, and rolled out into the open. She'd lost her rifle on initial impact, and her arms and legs flopped once, then lay still and useless.

Concurrently with the camouflaged markswoman's tumble, rifle fire erupted all around the edge of the woods and the less-wooded valley beyond. The crowd ahead was breaking apart in a panic. In the chaos of the immediate moment, it was impossible to determine exactly what the hell was going on.

The shots came from multiple positions. Some of them seemed to be shooting at Ty, and he ducked back down through the hatch to take advantage of the truck's armored body and reinforced windshield.

Other riflemen were shooting elsewhere, and if Ty wasn't mistaken, they were targeting the very shooters trying to take him out. A battle had broken out between two opposing groups of snipers, all of them hidden in the trees and rocks that overlooked the valley entrance.

Crackling gunfire drowned out the shouts, screams, and general rustling of the massed farmers. At least two rifle rounds struck the Autocutioner and set the metal to briefly *ring* and vibrate as the projectiles shattered or ricocheted off.

Ty kept his head down all the same. The windshield was strong enough to resist a lot of punishment, but he didn't know what calibers the shooters were using. A sufficiently large and powerful round might punch right through. A repeated barrage of more middling calibers could have the same effect.

Still, he had no intention of staying where he was. He'd sought safety only for the moment it would take him to assess the situation—then jump into action.

The crowd was fragmenting. The villagers had no idea what was going on or how to deal with it and ran wildly in all directions. Quite a few raced toward the Autocutioners.

The direness of that fact impressed itself immediately upon Ty's brain. If he were to dismount from the vehicle, he would have to fight the human flood to accomplish anything. He didn't like hanging back on the edge of a scrap. It was in his nature to be right in the center of the maelstrom. Right now, he would do more good where he was at.

He poked his head and shoulders back out of the hatch. His rifle came up beside him and sought out a target. Any target. He spied a flash about two hundred yards away to his left. It looked as though the unknown shooter there was firing at someone else on the valley's opposite side, not at Ty, his friends, or the farmers.

"What the hell?" he lamented. "I don't even know what's going on." He glanced down at Gage, Dante, and their prisoners. His eyes widened.

Tilda Ashcroft had seen her opportunity and taken it.

The instant someone passed between herself and Gage, she bolted deeper into the crowd, ducking, lunging, and striking out as needed. She targeted faces with her elbows or fingertips and groins with her feet, stunning anyone who got in her way as she moved toward her brother.

Hugh had moved away from Dante amid the general brouhaha, but Dante already struggled after him. Tilda reached her brother first, though, grabbing him by the arm and pulling him through the narrow space between two small clusters of farmers.

Then two men went down almost perfectly in unison, although the timing was coincidental. One farmer was struck in the head by a stray rifle bullet, blood spurting from his ear as he collapsed flat on his back. The other fell over due to Tilda and Hugh pummeling him in the face and neck while kicking his legs.

Both men carried weapons. The Ashcrofts took them. Tilda ended up with a one-handed sickle, while Hugh seized a two-handed wood-splitting ax. Before darting toward the far side of the crowd where no one was, least of all the Executioners, Hugh paused to swing the ax's blade into the fallen farmer's chest before ripping it free.

Ty trembled in rage. Even his long experience in combat and desperate situations couldn't completely inoculate him against the rising sense of frustration that verged on panic. Everything had gone wrong, and so far, there was little he could do about it.

Sensing someone's eyes on him again, he ducked back into the hatch in time to evade another rifle shot that *dinged* and sparked off the hull next to the opening. Then he had to trust that the sniper might be taking fire from one of the opposing riflemen, having given away their position.

Ty popped back up and trained his AR-10 on the Ashcrofts. Their experience with hunting had given them a disturbingly adept sense of how to move through a landscape that was dense with obstacles. They crouched behind logs and stumps, moved in unpredictable zigzags, and protected themselves behind innocent bystanders whenever they could. It was all but impossible to get a clear shot at either of them.

Daria had the same idea. Being closest to the two since she'd already been toward the center of the scene and wasn't jostled back by fleeing locals, she'd set off in swift pursuit. Her pistol was out of its holster and held at low ready in her hands. Each time she tried to raise it to bring the murderous brother and sister down, though, she ran into the same problems Ty did.

The crowd refused to clear out. The hidden snipers continued to take potshots at the assembled locals, or at least to pull their shots and send stray bullets into their midst. In their panic, the farmers kept running back and forth, essentially clogging the whole area as they tried to get away from threats that came from multiple directions without apparent rhyme or reason.

When another shot drove a group of half a dozen terrified people right in front of Daria, Hugh, and Tilda, Ty decided to try something different. He raised his rifle and aimed for the trees.

It seemed that there was at least one marksman out there who was on his side—or at least, who had a common enemy. But his first loyalty was to the other Executioners and to the fulfillment of their duties.

He switched to full auto and sprayed bursts into the seemingly-empty stretches of wilderness all around them from where the rifle reports seemed to be coming or where he'd seen muzzle flashes erupting. The barrages of lead shook the leaves and tore thinner branches off while drawing out clouds of sawdust. No bodies toppled, though.

It was unlikely he'd hit anything. That wasn't the point. The sniper fire stopped for the moment, giving the people on the ground a measure of peace to reposition themselves.

Ty cast a glance down and ahead. The good news was that most of the crowd had filtered away from Daria, Hugh, and Tilda. Ms. Barruk was catching up to the fleeing pair, who furthermore were up against the base of a steep ridge.

The bad news was that at least two dozen people, more than half of the overall assemblage from the valley, had milled toward the Autocutioners, getting in Gage's and Dante's way. They both shouted and barked orders at the farmers to clear a path and stand aside, but it took too long for the civilians to get the message.

There was no way they could get to Daria before she had to take on both of the Ashcrofts by herself.

Ty ejected his empty magazine and slammed in another as Daria raised her Browning toward Hugh to gun him down. Ty saw with a sinking feeling that she was relying upon the goodwill and intelligence of a hysterical nearby woman. The woman ducked between the Executioner and her prey, ruining the shot at the last second.

While Daria tried to step around to the side to regain her sight picture, Tilda came up around the other woman's flank, charging in and flailing her sickle.

Daria pivoted and fired a single shot, which went over Tilda's shoulder. Then Hugh came toward her with his ax. By a stroke of awful luck, Daria was directly between him and Ty's rifle.

"Goddammit, Daria, get out of the way!" As good as Ms. Barruk was, the whole situation had degenerated into such a fiasco that everyone struggled merely to stay on top of things. There was no time to execute a well-ordered plan.

Then another rifle shot whizzed by his head, narrowly missing his left eye as he slightly adjusted his position. "Shit!" He ducked in time to avoid a second shot. When he looked out the windshield from within the vehicle, a gaping pit opened in his stomach.

Hugh and Tilda had worked together and used the general anarchy to their advantage. They'd swarmed Daria and overcome the advantage of having only melee weapons instead of her gun. Tilda swiped the sickle over Daria's forearm, cutting the back of her hand and catching the pistol from behind to yank it from her grasp. Then Hugh moved in to hammer her in the stomach with the blunt side of his ax.

"No!" Ty exclaimed. He froze, uncertain what to do—a rare occurrence for him.

By the time the last of the crowd cleared out, Tilda had wrapped the business end of her sickle around Daria's throat while holding her from behind, and Hugh had exchanged his ax for the Executioner's Browning. All three were inching toward Daria's vehicle.

Most of the clamor had died down, and Ty knew he would make an easy target of himself if he reemerged from the hatch. He didn't care.

He stood straight up, bringing his rifle to bear quicker than he would've thought. Almost instantly a bullet grazed the armored pad of his shoulder, not injuring him, but throwing his aim badly off. Then Hugh, Tilda, and Daria were half-hidden behind the other Autocutioner.

Ty dropped back into the front seating area, dizzy with rage. Diagonally ahead and to the side, Gage and Dante were still trying to push free from the press of bodies. Much of the crowd had gathered near the trucks for the extra cover they provided from the snipers. The rest of them had fled back toward their village.

Cursing his refusal to accept the situation for what it was, Ty kicked open the door, jumped down, and sprinted across the space between himself and Daria, weaving around the edge of the farmers and ignoring the possibility that a rifle might strike him down at any second.

"Tilda!" he snarled as soon as she, her brother, and their hostage came into full view. They'd squeezed into the narrow space beside the other Autocutioner's front end and a low hillock streaked with roots behind them.

Daria was the first to see him. Her expression looked drawn but not terrified. If anything, she was furious.

Then the Ashcrofts saw him. "Stop," Tilda ordered. "I'll cut her throat if you approach another step. This thing is quite sharp, but the edge is a bit ragged. It would be exceedingly messy."

Hugh chuckled. "I'll pick off one of the farmers at random. I'm not a bad shot with a pistol, you know."

Ty had already shouldered his rifle. It was aimed at his

nemeses before they'd spoken, so he didn't need to worry about scaring them into making good on their threats by raising the gun. Tilda's face was directly behind the front sight. However, Daria's was right next to it. Even the slightest fuck-up in his aim, and he would accomplish the exact opposite of what he meant to do.

"I have the drop on you," he barked. "Make the slightest move to hurt anybody, and you're both dead."

Tilda snorted. "We were dead to begin with. Don't you remember? What difference does it make to us? We care less about losing our lives than *you* care about your lady friend here, or for that matter the poor innocent peasants over there. Of course, what we would *prefer* is to get into that truck and drive away, all of us safe and sound."

If they sprang for the vehicle's door, he might not get them in time. They could kill Daria while they were at it. His chances didn't look good.

Ty's nostrils flared. "Take me instead, then. I'll go with you as a hostage. Let Daria go."

Hugh shook his head, and Tilda laughed with the same exaggerated unpleasantness she'd used so recently when mocking Gage's concern for her past.

"Hah! Why would I take the first of the Executioners when I can play with their heart instead? You said that yourself. She is your heart. A more vital organ. I have no idea which is the brain since none of you seem qualified for that role."

Daria's jaw fell open in exasperation. "Tyler! Just shoot this *pinda*. I'm tired of listening to her."

In speaking, she had managed to move her head an inch or two to the side. Just enough to provide a little clearance between her temple and Tilda's left eye.

Ty's finger started to squeeze the trigger.

The rifle that thundered first wasn't his. Something slammed into his chest, knocking him off his feet and flat on his back, his rifle falling from his grasp only to swing aside on its sling as he crashed into the ground. His torso felt as though it had emptied all at once. The bullet had struck right over his diaphragm and knocked every ounce of air from his lungs.

He struggled to sit up, but sudden asphyxiation and the onrush of pain made it all but impossible. He heard the doors of Daria's Autocutioner slam shut and Dante shouting incoherently somewhere behind him, along with screams and mutters from the crowd of locals.

Then the truck moved toward him.

He had no breath left to cry out. All he could do was flip himself over, rolling aside with about a second to spare as the huge wheels tore up the ground beside him and left him in their wake. The Ashcrofts were making good their escape, and Ty somehow doubted that Daria had slipped their grasp.

CHAPTER SEVEN

Through a tremendous effort of will, gritting his teeth and almost roaring with pain, Ty rolled himself around on his knees and rose halfway on one so he could spring into a standing position in a second. Standing wasn't the goal yet. His priority was telling Dante and Gage what to do before they did something stupid, like check on *him* instead of going after Daria.

As he'd feared, his friends were heading toward him. Gasping, he managed to choke out, "No, go after her! I'm fine." He flailed an arm weakly at the truck, which was already barreling up the road into the hills.

Dante hesitated for a second, but Gage ignored him and kept jogging Ty's way. Behind the two of them, the farmers were getting over their panicked timidity and starting to look angry. A few were stepping out front as though they intended to storm toward the Executioners and demand answers.

The hidden rifles had, for the time being, fallen silent. Ty wondered who they were. Tilda's and Hugh's benefactors must have hired them to help the pair escape. No other explanation made the slightest amount of sense.

How did the Ghost-Makers fit into it all?

Gage came up to Ty and slid an arm under his shoulder, bearing him up to stand. "Are you all right?"

"Mostly," Ty grunted. "It didn't get through my armor, just banged the shit out of me. Goddammit, you should be going after *them.*"

Then Dante was at his side as well, examining the front of his torso. "Hell of a dent. Looks like it got you right in the solar plexus. So you probably escaped any broken ribs or cracked sternum, but you might still have severe bruising, internal bleeding, a hernia, a traumatic ulcer, or a—"

"No," Ty insisted, clawing at the air in his terrible frustration, "I'm fucking *fine,* okay? They're getting away!"

Dante shook his head. "They *already* got away, boss man. Even if we'd decided to be bad friends and left you there, they had enough of a head start that it would be useless. Besides, our other buddies are surrounding Gage's truck. We'd have had to plow through them. I think they're only now regaining the use of their brains. We all need to get out of the line of fire, though. Those snipers might still try to take us all out."

Ty was having some trouble walking due to the minor trauma to his lower chest. Breathing again wasn't too easy. Gage continued to support him as they moved closer to the hill road, where rises in the earth would protect them from the bulk of the rifle fire that might sail in from the forest. Dante went in front.

Getting to the remaining Autocutioner was going to be tougher than any of them had anticipated. Once again, the farmers were in the way. Most of them had taken up positions in a skirmish line of sorts, two ranks deep, blocking the Executioners from their vehicle. The ones out in front were slowly advancing.

With the sniper fire ended, the *other* farmers were crossing the clearing as well. They were moving faster and with purpose.

All of them looked angry.

Gage mused, "Hmm. We might have a problem here, Tyler.

The community leaders appear to be upset over what has happened. They might blame us for it."

"What?" Ty scoffed. Even a cursory glance at the lines of faces massing around them suggested that Gage was right, of course, but he didn't want to accept it. It was one more complication they didn't have time to deal with, something that would get in the way of their pursuit of Daria and the Ashcroft twins.

Dante paused and allowed his friends to catch up. "Yeah, they don't look happy. Even though we were only here to do what they wanted and we might've saved them from ending up a lot worse. Still, they lost a couple of people. You can't blame them for being pissed. We don't have Daria around to talk our way out of this."

By the time the trio had covered half of the distance to Gage's Autocutioner, the villagers near the vehicle had formed a half-circle to envelop them as they approached. The others, approaching from the rear at greater speed, were in a position to cut off any attempted retreat into the valley.

Their only options were to deal with the farmers—which might entail having to go *through* them—or to attempt to scale one of the slopes to the side, which would have been a dicey proposition even if Ty weren't injured.

Ty scanned the people before them. They were frightened, enraged, and irrational. He could tell that much in an instant. Their hostility was still more or less of a *defensive* variety, or so it seemed to him. There was still a chance of defusing the tensions.

"All right, halt," he said in a ragged voice to his companions. "Let's try to reason with them."

A fiftyish man in front of the crowd, armed with a hoe, stopped. His face was an ugly mask of negative emotions—anger, fear, grief, and what looked a lot like the hurt of betrayal.

"You bastards!" he bellowed. "You brought this on us. We lost three good people. Why? What the hell are you doing, getting us shot at?"

Ty glanced aside. In addition to the man whom Tilda and Hugh had killed, two others had been struck down by bullets from the hidden rifles.

Before he or his partners could respond, a dozen other farmers echoed the apparent leader's accusation, throwing in wordless screams of irrational dismay and waving their weapons.

Dante sighed, "Crap. This isn't going well so far. Especially since we don't have a good answer for them, do we?"

Gage remarked in a low voice, "Do not admit that we knew there were assassins after us. We must explain to them that it came as a surprise."

When they tried to tell their side of the story, though, the farmers simply shouted over them. They'd experienced too much pain and fear lately. The extra violence that had occurred today had pushed them past their breaking point, and they needed a target for their anger. Any target.

Some woman, probably the same one who'd insisted they execute the Ashcrofts in the town square, screamed, "We should string *you* up, instead!"

Ty felt his lips drawing slowly away from his teeth. He might still get a chance to fight today, in close quarters, no less. Still, he didn't want to hurt these people.

Plus, their odds weren't good. Despite their armor, training, and superior weapons, the three of them could do only so much against three dozen enraged adversaries. They might be able to take out a dozen before the farmers swarmed them. There was a slim chance they could break through the skirmish line and get to the abandoned Autocutioner with all of them still intact.

Ty whispered to Dante and Gage, "We might have to start shooting. When we do, make a break for the truck. The goal is to scare them away and *get* away. If they're that determined to kill us, make them fucking pay for it."

Gage exhaled. "I didn't wish for it to come to this."

As the mob moved closer, though, it was obvious from their nearly mouth-foaming bloodlust that they *did* wish for it.

Then the Autocutioner began to move forward. Everyone, Executioners and farmers both, froze in shock.

Ty's mind raced, and his thoughts jostled against one another. There were too many possibilities—too many different people who *might* be driving the vehicle and not enough time to parse them all out.

The first small group of locals turned to smack the truck's sides or shout obscenities at it. As it picked up speed, the others grasped that the driver meant to plow through them or run them over if need be. They flung themselves aside or were dragged to safety by their friends, unwittingly clearing a path between it and the beleaguered trio.

Dante marveled, "What the hell? Who's driving that thing?"

Ignoring his obvious and redundant question, Ty glanced at the windshield, but in the glare of the sun, all he could see was a dark human silhouette. His rifle was still up, but he didn't dare try to shoot the person behind the wheel. Powerful as it was, the AR-10 might not reliably puncture the heavy material and ricochets could be dangerous to him as well as the farmers.

There was always the chance that whoever had hijacked the truck was on their side.

Gage pointed. "The back door is open. Shall we try to get in?"

The Autocutioner had picked up speed to scare off the farmers, but as it drew closer to the three, it slowed down. Not enough for it to come to a complete stop, but enough that they could probably jump into the rear compartment without too much trouble.

Ty ran a hand over his midsection, drew a deep breath, and twisted his torso to both sides. The pain was still there, but it wasn't as bad as it had been. He wasn't too badly hurt.

"Yeah," he replied. "We don't have much choice, do we? Unless the driver is trying to ram us. I don't think they are."

The hostile agriculturists who'd been the first to disperse when the truck had first moved were now jogging toward them again, yelling and waving their crude weapons. The ones closer to them were too busy getting out of the way, but they still looked angry enough to resume the lynch mob once they recovered.

The truck swung around in a gentle curve, nearly broadsiding a handful of locals who'd charged toward it with their pitchforks and hatchets, and the opened back compartment was only two yards from the three men.

Dante, the youngest and tallest of them, ran and jumped. He easily cleared the bumper and wobbled on the edge, then turned, crouched, and reached out a hand.

Gage was still supporting Ty, who pushed him off. "I'm fine. You go next."

Dante's hand clasped Gage's, hoisting the small man up, and the Nepali caught a metal rim and pulled himself in as Ty prepared a dive of his own. In two seconds, the truck—which hadn't stopped moving—would be out of range.

Both of his friends extended their arms. Ty took a short running start, his feet pounding the ground three times before he launched himself at the space before him.

Dante and Gage caught him, but the force of the jump was enough that he slipped through their grasp and crashed onto the metal floor beyond them. His chest plate struck the hard surface and pressed against his diaphragm, leaving him gasping in pain and cursing between gritted teeth.

Before the others could close the back door, the truck picked up speed. It continued to drive in a semicircle, essentially doubling back toward the valley, shooting past the infuriated villagers and into the open grassy area between the hills and the farming community proper. The driver was taking them toward the jungle road.

Whoever they were, they weren't wasting time about it. It was practically miraculous that none of the farmers had been rammed or run over. Ty wondered if that was intentional. He couldn't tell if the individual behind the wheel was actively trying to avoid casualties or was simply indifferent to them one way or another.

While Gage shut the door, Dante knelt beside Ty. "You okay? Christ, it looked like you were trying to *break through* the truck instead of jumping into it."

"Oh," Ty grumbled, sitting up, "I'm as close to perfect as I'll ever be. Help me up."

Dante took his arm and lifted him to his feet. Gage came up beside them as the sunlight from the vehicle's rear gave way to shadows, and all of their faces turned toward the interior door separating the back compartment from the front seating area.

It was time to find out who their mysterious savior was.

Ty stepped forward. The pain was receding again, more quickly this time than it had the first time around. "I'll go first. Watch me."

Gage and Dante fell in behind him at his flank. Both of them drew their handguns while Ty kept his right hand resting on the hilt of his wakizashi. With his left hand, he flung open the door, exposing the front cockpit area for all to see.

It was a woman. None of the three had ever seen her before.

She looked back at them with an expression that was simultaneously intense and cool. She was paying close attention to everything around her but was in control of herself and her emotions. Nothing about her demeanor suggested ill intent, but she didn't exactly look friendly either.

Ty pulled himself through the doorway and stood braced in a half-crouch behind her and to the side, occupying the space between the seats, holding onto one with his free left hand.

"Who are you?" he asked.

The woman had already turned her head forward again, watching the road as she drove. She had short, wiry black hair and gleaming skin of deep ebony, with a patchy scar on her right cheek and a line scar on her chin. It was difficult to guess her age with any degree of accuracy. She was past adolescence but not yet "old" by any stretch of the imagination.

Ty couldn't see much of her body shape since she wore a green camouflage poncho over her shoulders. Beneath it, she appeared to be wearing safari-type gear, with well-worn knee-length shorts and rugged hiking boots.

A suspicion occurred to him, but Ty didn't entertain it yet. His best estimate, so far, was that the woman was a member of the village community who'd resisted the mindless undertow of mob vengeance and decided to help the Executioners rather than risk their wrath.

Up ahead, the trees, ferns, and brush of the encroaching jungle were growing closer. The angry locals were too far behind to try anything.

The woman's full lips parted as though she were about to answer Ty's inquiry, but she was trying to choose her words carefully and hesitant to speak. Not out of fear, it seemed, but simply out of a desire to get it right.

Dante had come up front and squeezed into the space between Ty and the door. He tapped Ty's shoulder and pointed toward the passenger seat.

Resting there with its butt on the floor and its lower frame against the edge of the seat was a Remington Model 700 marksman rifle, complete with an attached bipod and a scope. The faint smell of burned gunpowder indicated that the driver had recently fired it.

That confirmed Ty's lurking suspicion.

His wakizashi flashed from its scabbard, cutting through the side of the passenger seat in the tight quarters as Ty practically exploded with rage. Before the blade could complete its arc into the woman's throat, a hand clamped onto Ty's arm, holding it in place with surprising strength.

"Wait!" Gage's voice insisted. "We must find out who she is. Please, let us talk to her first."

Dante, too, had moved closer to Ty—to grab his other arm if necessary, but also to protect him in case the strange woman stopped driving for long enough to strike back.

She did not, however. A brief flick of her eyes indicated that she saw what had happened, and they all felt a momentary jolt of tension from her, but she relaxed again in an instant once it was clear that Ty's friends were holding him back from harming her. Otherwise, she didn't seem particularly distressed. It was as though such things were a common occurrence for her.

Ty froze, his brain still burning with the residues of his frustrated rage during the battle in the valley, while his midsection likewise burned with the physical pain of being shot.

Dante commented, "Gage is right. We don't know whose side she's on yet. Plus, she's the one driving the truck. Taking her head off would be a good way to crash us into a tree right when it looks like we're about to get away."

They'd passed beyond the valley's rim and were barreling into the countryside around the road Dante and Daria had taken from the city. The terrain wasn't as rugged as what Gage and Ty had driven over, but it was still rougher than the flat expanse of the agricultural vale behind them and dense with the foliage of the Atlantican rainforest.

Perversely enough, Ty felt like crying. He sucked air between his teeth and willed himself back to calm, killing the strange urge before it could become a reality. It was the sense of helplessness, he realized. The fact that he'd failed to do much of anything useful in the predicament they'd escaped and couldn't vent his grievances by shooting or stabbing anyone.

So far.

His friends were correct. He eased out of his killing stance and returned his sword to its scabbard. The woman would live, for now. She would also talk if she wanted to keep on living.

Before anyone could speak further, though, the radio crackled.

Gage released Ty's arm and stepped through the space between seats, settling himself on the passenger's side. "I will answer it. Please, madam, keep driving. We will not hurt you. Tyler, Dante, please stay where you are."

"Sure," Dante said. "To be honest, I kind of hate talking on the radio. No body language. Makes everything harder if you ask me."

Ty stood in silence, still braced against the driver's seat, as Gage flicked the switch and removed the microphone. He couldn't greet the person on the other end or ask what they wanted, however. The voice began its pitch the instant the device was engaged.

"Good day. It seems fair to assume that you're all safe and well, despite the unfortunate loss of your heart." Despite the faint static distortion, Tilda Ashcroft's voice was impossible not to recognize.

Ty stared at the radio. He'd readjusted his mental posture and was back in control of himself, which was good since his first impulse was to draw his sword again and split the radio in two.

He snapped, "Shut that off. Now."

"Wait," Gage protested. He covered the microphone with his hand, muffling it. "Please be calm, Tyler. Allow me to talk with her. There must be something she wants. Even for one such as her, it would be pointless to contact us for no reason except to gloat. She might have information we can use to help Daria."

Dante had remained aloof at first, but now he snapped his fingers. "Right, yeah. Let's hear what the little hussy and her loathsome brother have to say. If nothing else, they'll probably tell us if Daria's still alive."

Ty drummed his fingers on the grip of his wakizashi. "You're giving those two far more credit than I would. I doubt anything they say can be trusted or believed, and nothing they seem to want is rational or sane. But, fine. Talk to them, Gage. I'll shut up for the time being."

He waited.

Gage uncovered the microphone and spoke. "Yes, hello. We are here. What do you wish to talk about?" His tone was neutral, verging on friendly, and the small man himself was utterly calm. Ty marveled at how even-tempered the Gurkha was. He was probably the second-best qualified to negotiate after Daria.

"I wish," Tilda said, and for a couple of seconds it sounded as though she would trail off, "I wish to talk about what my brother and I intend to do and the favors we might appreciate from you people."

Gage said, "Of course."

Ty almost snapped at him to ask about Daria, but Tilda herself answered the query preemptively.

"Your friend is still alive thus far. We're taking her into the jungle. You won't know exactly where, of course. Somewhere we doubt you've been. For the time being she is safe and sound. Isn't that right, Ms. Barruk?"

Daria shouted, "Fuck off! This charade is stupid. You..." she switched to a stream of Polish. Ty recalled having heard some of it amid other tirades of English profanity that Daria had used during some of her more animated moments.

Hugh Ashcroft laughed somewhere in the background, a droll, hollow chuckle, as though amused by a child's attempt to explain some natural phenomenon in nonsense terms.

His sister regained control of the microphone. "So yes, she is unmarked so far. Anyone foolish enough to follow us can expect to discover the full range of our creativity. We will do terrible, *terrible* things to her if we have any reason to believe someone is pursuing us. Recall that we were willing to do such things to persons who technically deserved them *less* than she did if you doubt our resolve."

"Oh," Ty muttered under his breath, "I don't."

Ignoring him, Gage said, "We are heading in a different direction. What else would you like us to know?"

Ty nodded at that. The casual way Gage had declared as much made it sound more like the truth, which it was, rather than a desperate lie. At the same time, he'd neglected to give the siblings any information about exactly where they *were* going.

Tilda laughed in a short, haughty way. "Well, isn't that comforting. Now, then. If you don't want to see the results of our creativity on your lady friend, you'll appreciate our desire to take our show back on the road. To put it simply enough for simple minds to comprehend—we'd like to get a few things in order, then we want to escape. In exchange for your services in this endeavor, we'll trade Ms. Daria Barruk back to you. Relatively undamaged."

Ty expelled air from his nostrils and tried not to distract himself with fantasies of splitting the Ashcrofts' skulls open.

Fortunately, Gage was still the one doing the talking. "We understand, yes. Please allow me to talk about it with my team, and we will have a decision for you soon."

"Oh, but I would hurry," Tilda suggested, her voice thick with mock concern. "With all the shooting recently, it seems that you Executioners have other problems, don't you? With blood in the water, you can bet that the sharks will be circling."

Hugh chuckled again, then said, "Out. For now."

Gage hung up the receiver. He stared at his friends, and they stared back, trying to judge how many of each other's thoughts they could read or anticipate.

Dante was the first to break the silence. "Okay. So they want us to help them get out of here so they can be pieces of human filth somewhere else, I get it. What the hell do they want us to *do*, though? What's this crap about getting Daria back *relatively* undamaged? That can mean a lot of different things. I'm a doctor. I would know."

Despite his slightly flippant choice of words, Dante's worry for his coworker and his barely suppressed wrath at her captors was undeniably genuine. His dark eyes blazed, and he kept running a hand through his backswept hair.

Ty said, "Who the fuck knows? They might keep changing the terms of the deal as we go, stringing us along again and again, and still renege at the last minute. Tilda lied to us about half of her background for the fun of it. These people don't inhabit the same reality we do. They were so bored with their safe, indulgent lives as children that they would do something like that to *entertain* themselves and think nothing of it.

"I'd say the best thing we can do is play along with their little game for the time being. At least we can buy time for ourselves. And for Daria."

Gage folded his leathery hands in front of himself and gave a slow nod. Ahead of them, the emerald fronds of the woods had grown denser, plunging the day into the jungle's artificial twilight.

"I agree," the Gurkha declared. "There is another thing we must consider. There might be a great, ah, what is the term? Lashing back? If the word gets out about this. People will react badly if they discover that we negotiated with these people we were to execute. It will make us look weak. The people of the farming valley will say that we're untrustworthy."

Dante smacked the back of the passenger's seat. "Goddammit. You're right. Oh, and it's 'backlash,' one word. Maybe we can play along for now. We have to resolve this thing quickly before it gets out of hand."

They sat without speaking for a long moment, each man alone with his thoughts despite the close presence of his friends.

Then the driver spoke up. They'd all nearly forgotten she was there.

"I know what Tilda Ashcroft is really up to," she proclaimed. "I can help you."

The faces of all three Executioners snapped toward her. She

turned a calm glance toward them to ensure she had their attention before looking back at the road and continuing to pilot the truck deeper into the wilderness.

Dante raised his eyebrows. "Oh? Go on."

"I can help you," the woman repeated. Her accent was odd, probably African but with a definite European influence, suggesting that she'd lived under one of the colonial regimes. "But I want to make a deal."

Ty's eyes bulged. The blinding hot fury was back. He snapped, "The fact that you're still *breathing* is a hell of a better deal than I give most people who've taken a shot at me."

Unfazed, the woman continued to work the steering wheel, waiting for the other two men to add their commentary. When she glanced aside again, it wasn't at any of them but at her rifle. She was checking to ensure that Gage hadn't carelessly knocked it over when he'd climbed into the seat.

Dante cleared his throat. "Mr. Katakura might have a short temper, but he has a point. If you were one of the people shooting at us, why are you suddenly our friend?"

Gage added, "What is the deal you wish to make, madam?"

The sniper kept her eyes on the road, but her tone grew sharper. "I know where they are *not* heading, and I also know what they plan to do. You will find out only with my help. If Daria is delivered back to you because of my actions, this is what I expect from you—I want to be made an Executioner."

CHAPTER EIGHT

Ty's solar plexus seemed to scream in rage all by itself, without his mind having to prompt it.

"Sorry," he hissed, in the same tone of voice he would've used to pronounce a death sentence. "We're not recruiting at the moment." His right hand rested on his sword hilt.

The vibe within the truck had shifted to one of subdued hostility and awkward discomfort.

Gage explained, "Madam, to be an Executioner is far more than only a title or membership in a gentlemen's club. Or ladies' club. It comes with responsibilities of a most serious nature."

"Responsibilities and costs," Dante added. His face was grim, yet also distant and sorrowful. Noticing the look and the way his eyes darkened, Gage guessed that he must've been thinking about Janet, the woman he'd tried to love.

The Nepali looked back at the scarred woman behind the wheel. "Yes, costs which we take most seriously. It's not as though you're applying for a paper route. You must understand that we have to know your qualifications. Why should we take your word that you're fit for the position?"

The African woman's face slowly distorted, looking like a

frown, which transformed into something much like a snarl. Then, abruptly, she laughed. "Hah!"

Her foot slammed on the brakes. The vehicle jerked and jostled, the brakes grinding and squealing as the tires spun in the soft, muddy earth and the massive vehicle veered halfway off the road to stop mere inches from a fat green tree.

The woman had buckled her safety belt. The men had not. The impact of the sudden halt nearly threw Gage from his seat over the dashboard. Dante fell against the right wall of the front compartment and Ty against the left. His hand fumbled for his sword since he was sure she was about to try either killing them or fleeing the vehicle and leaving them in the lurch.

She did neither. Once the Autocutioner was stationary, she only sat in place and waited for the trio to regain their balance. Then she turned and looked at Ty, her face fierce and proud. When she spoke, the words came out fast and sharp in a torrent calibrated to overwhelm them and permit no word to come in edgewise.

"Do not disappoint me with such foolishness! Asking for my qualifications when I have information that you do not. Information that can save your friend, this woman Daria. Is that a qualification? Ability to save her life? That should say something. As well, I saved you from an angry mob that you couldn't deal with by yourselves. Your qualifications for such things would seem to be less than mine, would they not?"

Dante raised a finger, and Gage blinked. Ty only stared. She was looking around at each of them in turn, but at last, she settled on staring back at him.

"It doesn't end there," she continued. "For I have also saved you from the Ghost-Makers, who would've had all your heads without me. You walked straight into their trap with no idea of the danger you were in. I was a member of them! I would know. It was only my actions that spared you from death. And that was not the beginning of it!"

Slowly, she extended a dark, lean-muscled arm toward Tyler. She had no weapon in hand; she was merely gesturing toward him. He was nevertheless prepared to *remove* her hand the instant she made a wrong move.

Nonetheless, he listened. All of his attention was focused on her and the unexpected, rapid-fire verbal tirade she had unleashed upon them.

"Even before!" she went on. "Even before today, you blind fool. That other night at the chateau of those people. I saved your life at least twice. It was not only the stick. I broke it! I alerted you. I was the one who shot that man within the house, who would have killed you otherwise. Do you understand, now, at last? If nothing else, all of you owe me."

Her voice deepened, hardened, and became a solemn pronouncement, and her hand uncurled so that a single finger pointed at Ty's chest. "You in particular, sir."

Tyler Katakura had gone still. He held her gaze, not flinching from it but still unsure how to react. The force and confidence of her response had taken him aback, and her insinuations demanded further thought.

There was no way in this place and at this time to verify the truth of her words. No way to prove she'd been at the hunting lodge, secretly guiding the course of the battle to spare him assassination.

Someone had certainly been there. He'd told nobody except his fellow Executioners. Not to mention, there was the matter of the first sniper in the tree today—the one who was half a second from blowing Ty's head off when someone else had shot her.

If even a third of what the strange woman had said was veritable and accurate, she deserved their attention. And perhaps their gratitude.

Ty looked at his partners. Both Dante and Gage were watching him, waiting for his response. The woman had spoken primarily to *him*, after all, and they tended to defer to him, the first Executioner, when in doubt. Still, he tried to read their faces.

Gage's was calm, as usual. His eyes were wide and attentive, and his open, almost friendly demeanor suggested that he hoped Ty would humor the woman and deal with her graciously.

Dante squinted in uncertainty. He was skeptical about the whole thing, yet he didn't appear to consider himself qualified to intrude or to override whatever decision Tyler was about to come to.

Ty looked back at their hidden benefactor. She was right about one thing, namely, that he owed her his life. Did he owe her a job? Could a wild card, an unknown, a potential loose cannon be allowed into their order? Was the potential sabotage of everything the Executioners stood for worth the information that might save the life of Daria Barruk—his best friend?

That was the complicated part. He hated complications. He drew a deep breath.

"We will accept your deal," he said, with a slow, single nod. "But if Daria does not come back to us alive, I will kill you myself."

There was a flash behind her eyes, like that which preceded sudden violence, but the woman's self-control was good. Which, in a way, made her even more dangerous. People who could master their emotions while remaining defiant in the face of a killer like Tyler Katakura were not to be trifled with.

"I agree." She gestured with her head toward the radio. "To save her life, it would be better that you hurry. The crazy woman and her brother might've grown impatient. Or simply bored. They have strange ways of dealing with their boredom."

Ty looked at his partners. Dante was eyeing the woman with not-so-vague suspicion. Gage was already reaching for the device to call Tilda back, so Ty couldn't get a good view of his face.

Gage unhooked the receiver and flicked the switch. It was unnecessary to adjust the frequency since they were still on the same as the other Autocutioner. "Hello. Tilda? Hugh? We have reached our decision."

Tilda's voice responded in perhaps a second and a half at most. "Oh, really? This ought to be interesting."

The Gurkha cleared his throat. "We have accepted your offer. In exchange for Daria not being harmed and you returning to us, we will help you and work with you as much as we can. Over."

On the other end, both Ashcroft siblings laughed in unison, the tone an unpleasant mixture of intentional mockery and organic mirth. They legitimately found Gage's response funny.

"Oh, that's rich," Tilda drawled. "Of course, you would *say* that. Perhaps you even mean around half of it. Let's not kid ourselves, shall we? We *know* that you're trying to come up with some way or another of double-crossing us. It's the way such things work.

"*But let me remind you,*" her voice took on an edge and became nearly guttural, "that your friend's life is at stake. Her existence is in our good hands. You should therefore be very careful in planning your treacheries because we'll be very careful in planning our vengeance. Is that clear?"

Gage's frown betrayed the fact that even he was growing tired of Tilda's taunting histrionics. "Yes, it is clear. Let us know that Daria is still okay, please. Over."

Daria started to shout something but was then muffled after the first expulsion of sound, as though someone had clamped a hand over her mouth.

Tilda cut in. "Yes, yes, she is fine. I'm glad you're capable of seeing reason. So. Stay out of the jungle. You have no business anywhere in the wilderness. Not in the hills, not in the forest beyond the hills, nowhere. Remove yourselves and your truck to your clubhouse in Atlantica Metro and stay there. Wait for us to call you."

Gage looked up at Ty, who nodded.

"Yes," the Nepali conceded. "We are headed back to the city now. Over."

Tilda went on, "We still have friends in Atlantica, you know. They will see if you are dallying. So for your sake, and your friend's, do please hurry. Because if I don't receive confirmation that you people are where you're supposed to be, well, you'll leave us with no choice. Hugh will have to slip something into Daria, an inch for every minute past the time we expect to hear from you. No matter where that statement took your imaginations, you must surely understand how much Daria will appreciate your punctuality."

Then the radio cut out. No sign-off or any further words at all; nothing. The Ashcrofts had shut it down. They felt nothing more needed to be said.

"Fuck," Ty exclaimed. He felt like he wanted to throw up. Daria had been in danger before since he'd known her, but nothing like this. She'd never been reduced to a mere hostage and threatened with unspeakable torments and violations, dependent on the rest of them for help. He felt as helpless to do anything about it as he had during the firefight less than half an hour ago.

Dante, too, was cursing up a storm and driving his fist against the truck's inner metal lining. "Those bags of shit. Goddammit. What the hell do they think we are, job interviewers? Telling us to go home and wait for them to call? The hell with this!"

Gage, to the surprise of his friends, was done pretending to be amiable and affectless. His hands trembled with rage and his eyes burned. With a hard, almost murderous expression, he looked at the woman behind the wheel, drawing her gaze.

"You," he began. "You said you had information that will help us. Talk, and talk quickly. We do not have much time. First, we will have your name."

Surprised by the ice in his voice, Ty and Dante fell silent and turned to watch the exchange between him and their new partner.

The woman wore the same expression of intense focus combined with apparent calm, but Ty recognized that her cool exterior was cracking. At last, she'd realized that however formidable she might be at long range with a .308 at her fingertips, she was now within arm's reach of three men who were willing and able to kill her if she made them sufficiently angry. She seemed too smart to dismiss or fail to acknowledge the mounting danger of her situation.

"My name is Amahle Nikoze," she began. "I am Nguni Xhosa, from South Africa. I know all of your names."

Ty nodded. "I'm sure you do, Amahle. We're celebrities these days. Now, talk."

She obliged, her demeanor softening a little. Her words once more came out in a rapid deluge, but she enunciated well enough that it was easy to follow the flow.

"The Ghost-Makers to whom I belonged. At first, the group of so-called hunters, to which Tilda and Hugh belonged, were the ones who hired us. They requested our services and agreed to pay handsomely for them. What they wanted, as you might guess, was to eliminate you, Executioner Katakura. They knew that you would be coming for them soon."

Ty grunted. "Yeah. I figured as much. You said 'at first.' What does that mean? What happened next? Oh, and since time is precious, start driving again. I'm sure you can drive and talk."

Amahle started the engine and pulled the truck back onto the road. It rumbled over the soft earth and knocked aside branches and fronds on its course through the jungle. The woman continued to speak at a rapid clip, regaling them with the strange turns her organization's fortunes had taken since initially drawing up the contract.

As they made their preparations to ensnare and assassinate Ty, another party contacted them—only a day later—with goals of their own. Objectives that contradicted and intertwined with those of the hunting cabal. They wanted *everyone* dead.

"These people, through their contact," Amahle elaborated, "wished for us to leave no one alive at the lodge. They wanted you to die along with them, everyone together, so it would appear as though you killed them all, only to succumb to your wounds at the end and fail to make it out in time to seek treatment. That way, there would be no great investigation. The entire thing would become a dead end. For this, they were willing to pay a tremendous price."

Dante leaned closer. "Let me guess, you never saw anyone's face or heard them mention any names. It was all done in complete anonymity, and you have zero information for us on who this second party was. Am I right?"

A faint smile played at the corner of Amahle's mouth as though she were impressed by the tall physician's sudden display of wit. "Yes, that is correct."

Gage pressed on with, "So, you were still a member of the Ghost-Makers when they took this contract. You left them only a few days ago, at most. Tell us the rest."

Amahle confirmed this and did as asked, relaying as much information as possible in an abbreviated time.

Something was wrong, she felt, the instant the second group demanded that they betray the people they'd agreed to work for. It went against their organization's principles in more ways than one.

First of all, the original contract was shady enough to begin with. It had been obvious to Amahle from the beginning that the "hunting lodge" was composed of people who were either crazy, deeply amoral or both. To take out a hit on an Executioner was no small matter. On Atlantica, the Executioners—and particularly Ty—were widely feared and greatly respected.

"The reason we decided to take them up on their offer, after some deliberation, was because it would appear that Katakura had become a martyr. He would die, but his reputation would remain intact," Amahle stated.

Ty smiled grimly. "Thanks. I'll take small favors over none at all. Go on. There's still a lot of important stuff you haven't cleared up yet. The goddamn clock is ticking."

She snapped, "I'm getting to that." She explained that the reversal job didn't sit well with her. Never before had they backstabbed an employer in such a fashion. By accepting the terms offered by the second party, they would be reneging on the first for no truly good reason. Only money.

Amahle sighed. "It is true that we were professionals, which is to say, that we have always expected payment for our work. We also had our principles. Knowing that my brothers and sisters would sell themselves out in such a way... It was too much for me.

"I tried to bring it up when the Ghost-Makers convened again and to urge them to think twice. It would taint us, I said. It would damage our reputation for absolute reliability, and it would also damage our souls. They wouldn't listen."

The group's leader, in particular, was adamant about fulfilling *both* contracts. Said leader was none other than the woman who'd plummeted from the tree before she could shoot Ty.

Dante folded his arms. "Well, she's dead now, anyway."

"I wouldn't be so sure of that," Amahle countered. "I couldn't find her body as I was sneaking to your truck."

Ty, Gage, and Dante all looked at one another in surprise. Then they looked back at Amahle.

Rather than elaborate upon the matter of her leader's recent fate, the South African returned to the point in her anecdote where she'd left off.

"The kickbacks would be greater from the second party, the one paying us to betray the first. Our leader would be the one who benefited the most. It was against our rules, our principles. She offered to share the profits with me. Or so she said. This, too, was a lie."

Ty pinched the bridge of his nose. "This is getting a little complicated for my tastes."

Amahle glared at him. "You were the one who wanted to hear *everything*. I'm giving you the fast and simple version."

Ty waved and told her to go on but keep leaving out the finer details. They only needed to know the broad strokes.

Amahle had spoken to the other Ghost-Makers one by one, in private, after the leader had made her overture. The leader was already laying the foundations to have Amahle kicked out of the outfit as soon as possible. At which point, there would no longer be any need to share the extra wealth with her.

She would be marked for death. Fair game.

"So," the woman concluded, "I came up with my plan at the end. I didn't have much time, but it was the best I could do. I thought that if I saved your life, it would prove my worth to you and the other Executioners. By joining your organization, I would receive protection from the Ghost-Makers. They would seek terrible vengeance against me otherwise. Especially after I put a defective bullet in our leader's gun."

The story added up, mostly. Ty had heard enough. His hands flexed, clenching and unclenching in growing impatience. "Fine, you don't want to die, so you'd rather join an organization like ours where everyone regularly puts themselves in mortal danger. I get it. Now, where are we going to find Hugh and Tilda?"

Amahle grimaced, obviously irritated at Ty's deadpan assessment of the Executioners' lifestyle, not to mention his implied jab at her courage.

She put her foot on the brake, but this time it was slower and more deliberate, as though she fully intended to stop here and wasn't doing it solely to make a point.

Ty looked out the windshield as well as the windows in each door. He didn't know exactly where the hell they were. The path Amahle had followed wasn't one he was familiar with, and he estimated that she'd taken a couple of turns as well, partially doubling back into the hills. They were near the jungle's edge, next to a tall and rising slope that led into the lower reaches of the mountains beyond.

Dante echoed the thoughts in his friends' heads. "Where are we, anyway?"

Amahle reached over and grabbed her rifle by the barrel. "Excuse me." Gage moved his legs aside as she slid the weapon across to her lap, taking it up in both hands but holding it low. Ty naturally tensed at the sight. There was no indication that she planned to attack them. She was simply gathering an important tool for future use.

Then with a smooth speed that was borderline alarming, the South African opened the driver's side door and hopped down to the ground.

"Come," she called over her shoulder. "I will show you."

Time was of the essence. Being led blindly into the unknown by a woman they had no specific reason to trust wasn't something Ty would've done under normal circumstances. Still, every minute wasted brought Daria closer to death and the Executioners closer to discredit and disgrace.

Ty grabbed up his things, made sure they were secure and turned to his friends, who were waiting on his lead.

Dante scoffed, "You're not seriously going to—"

"Get back to the bunker," Ty instructed, cutting him off. He'd fallen into the occasional habit of calling their headquarters the bunker although most of it was above ground. "Someone has to be there to await Tilda's call like she said. Be ready in case this whole miserable thing turns upside down on us."

Dante's jaw was hanging open, and his face stretched in an expression of total exasperation that bordered on comical.

Before he could protest, Gage, who'd remained neutral, said, "Yes, we will do that. Please be careful. Good luck."

Ty nodded. "Yeah. Let's hope this little deal with the devil works out."

CHAPTER NINE

Ty could still hear the Autocutioner rattling in the distance behind him as Gage drove it back to the city. Its clanking armor and grinding wheels were all but impossible to mistake, and the ambient sounds of the jungle weren't enough to mask them until sheer distance put it out of the range of his ears.

What he could *not* hear, though, was much of any noise made by Amahle Nikoze as she practically glided over the earth, passing through the foliage as though it wasn't there at all.

It was downright uncanny. Ty had spent no small amount of time in the bush, and the terrain here was some of the most difficult he'd ever encountered.

The woman's soft voice came down the slope toward him from somewhere up ahead within a swirling cloud of fog. "Here. This way. Move to the left, then back to the right."

"Yeah," he replied in an exaggerated whisper. Particularly with the vehicle's noises fading away, a hush fell over the wilderness. Silence seemed like the natural tendency, even without the nebulously hinted-at threat that someone or something unfriendly might hear them.

Ty's mood remained locked in the unpleasant mixture of simmering hostility, desperate frustration, and mounting tiredness that had afflicted him all day. It seemed he wouldn't get any respite or release. Fate, the gods, the powers of nature, or whatever they might be, were determined to test him and toy with him.

He'd prowled through the Atlantican rainforest before. Doing so for hours on end, not two full days ago, had been the prelude to his assault on the hunting cult's hidden mansion, after all. Since coming to the island, he'd spent much of his time on the frontier or embedded in the outright wilderness, creeping through all manner of terrain that seemed actively hostile to humans.

Each of those excursions differed from what he did now in one crucial way. He'd always had a plan. In every incident, he'd known in advance what he intended to do and more or less what awaited him. Plus, the fulfillment of each plan had been initiated by no one other than Tyler Katakura.

At present, he was being led into the depths of nowhere by a woman he'd known for less than an hour, on a mission whose objective was vague at best and whose dangers were unknown. He felt like he might as well be blindfolded, turned loose in a junkyard, and told to locate a particular piece of scrap metal by its color.

His jaw was getting tired from being clenched in irritation so often. His hands itched for the feel of his weapons when he *used* them. The way his rifle stormed in his hands when he fired it, the drag and resistance against his sword blade when he swiped it through flesh.

The fog was getting thicker. It was as much of an impediment to visibility and mobility as the jungle's plant life.

"Amahle?" he asked as he followed her instructions, veering back right after bearing left a moment ago. "Are you here?"

His feet had found a relatively clear path between two big

winding roots, and he guessed that it was the spot she'd intended for him to find. There was no way to be sure.

The South African's hushed voice reverberated down the slope. "Over here."

It sounded like she'd climbed farther up the hill while Ty had struggled to catch up with her. She'd moved slightly back to the left, as well.

The one good thing about the dense mist was that it made it harder to see Ty's flushed cheeks. He used to pride himself on his stealthy movements, bushcraft, and ability to move quickly and deftly over rough terrain. Back in the halcyon days, the golden age that had existed before this morning.

CHAPTER TEN

"Fuck!" he exclaimed as the round exploded against his armor, knocked him off his feet, and spun him around to twirl past the trunk of a tree and land facedown in a mass of moldy leaves.

The shock of being fired upon and the bullet's jarring impact filled his whole consciousness. By the time he hit the ground, he'd already regained enough presence of mind to begin calculating the shot's trajectory—and look around for cover.

The first thing his mind told itself, the most important fact, was that he wasn't dead or grievously wounded. His armor had protected him again. It had been a glancing blow, striking him from an acute angle that deflected more of the force than the shot he'd taken earlier. Still, his bruised midsection screamed with pain.

The second thing he noticed was Amahle reflexively diving for cover. Less than a second after the first shot had rung out—the instant the distinctive sound of a high-powered rifle had sundered the wilderness peace—she'd reacted on instinct, flinging herself amid the leaves and brambles of a nearby bush. The foliage wouldn't stop a bullet, but it would make her a hell of a lot harder to see.

Her body vanished into the mass of plant matter as two more shots rang out, kicking up explosions of dirt from the ground right behind where she'd been an instant ago. Had she been only marginally slower, the rounds probably would've punched through her chest or stomach.

The third and final thing that impressed itself upon his consciousness was the angle from which the hidden gunman had fired. The first shot had come at him obliquely. The sniper had tried to put a round through his chest at an angle, destroying his heart and tearing up his left lung for good measure.

The rounds he'd fired at Amahle had impacted the ground more closely behind her former position than they would've if he'd been on the same level as them. He was somewhere above them. Not *much* above, but definitely at a higher elevation, which was always ideal for shooting down unaware targets from cover.

He couldn't be too far. The vegetation was dense enough that no matter how good he was or what kind of high-grade scope he might have on his rifle, there was no way he could've seen them from a mile away.

Ty rolled over and brought up his rifle, pivoting the barrel toward the approximate spot where their hidden adversary seemed to have fired from. Then he squeezed the trigger and let off a short burst.

The gun roared like an injured beast, spewing six or seven rounds, and Ty let the muzzle climb a little and waved it around. He didn't intend to hit anything, only to put the sniper on the defensive long enough for himself and Amahle to react.

The jungle responded with total silence as the shots echoed into the distance. Ty seized the opportunity to crawl around the trunk of the nearby tree, putting it between his body and his unknown foe. It was a thick tree. It *might* have stopped a bullet in the three-oh-eight or thirty-aught-six range, but no guarantees. The important thing was that it would make it harder for the sniper to hit him. It rebalanced the odds in Ty's favor.

Within a second of the Executioner pulling himself into relative concealment, the sniper opened fire again. Two shots, fast enough on each other's heels that the marksman had to be using a semiautomatic rather than bolt-action rifle, exploded near where Ty had been. His burst of return fire had only highlighted his position.

The first round blasted up a cloud of muddy dirt a few feet past where Ty had lain seconds ago, similar to what had happened when the sniper had tried to shoot Amahle. The second bullet struck the tree.

Ty's breath hissed between his teeth. He felt the leaden chunk slam into the mass of wood in front of him—it sent a vibration all through it, and the thunderclap of the gun's report only faded gradually. The round didn't penetrate to the opposite side. Ty didn't doubt that it had blown a massive chunk out of the front.

His cover wouldn't last long.

It was enough to give him a moment to catch his breath and think logically. In Korea, they had plenty of ways of dealing with situations like this. The problem was that they all involved things like artillery, air support, or a substantially larger force than two people.

Even a squad might've been enough—ten or twelve guys could lay down enough firepower to potentially overwhelm the hidden rifleman through sheer volume of flying lead. Or they could've initiated a fire-and-maneuver sequence to keep their tormentor pressed down while some of them advanced and took him out.

He and Amahle would have to make do with all they had, which was each other and their pair of rifles. It wasn't much. It meant their chances weren't the best.

He might have to try storming the sniper's position by himself. If nothing else, the sheer brazen stupidity might confuse and overwhelm the man. Amahle could potentially help with suppressing fire.

Another shot rang out, again striking the tree trunk but failing to penetrate it fully. Ty looked back over his shoulder to the bush where Amahle had tossed herself. He could faintly see a dark, crouching silhouette beyond the lattice of branches.

So far, Amahle wasn't forthcoming with any suggestions for what to do or any activities that might get them out of this mess.

The sniper fired two more shots. One blew a fist-sized chunk from one of the thick roots near the tree's base, and another severed a low-hanging branch off to the side, mere inches from Ty's shoulder.

"Dammit," he breathed. He had no idea how much ammo the gunman had, but if it were any significant amount, he would eventually claim his prize through sheer attrition. Ty couldn't hide behind the tree indefinitely.

He scooched forward first on his rear then crawled on his belly, moving farther back from the trunk and into a lower spot of ground so the land itself plus the foliage would provide slightly more cover and concealment.

His mind raced. He'd bought himself a little time and extra room to maneuver. Still, he had to act quickly. If the sniper had any sense, he might well adjust his position, finding a different angle from which to shoot around the tree. Then Ty and Amahle both would be finished.

The best defense, as Ty had never failed to forget, was a good offense. He ejected his partially-spent magazine, pocketed it, and inserted a full one.

"Okay," he gasped, hopefully loud enough for Amahle to hear. "I'm going in." Another shot rang out, tearing up the earth a foot and a half beyond his thigh, and he sprang up, his AR-10 clutched in both hands and adrenaline surging.

He swung around the tree on the far end, giving Amahle room if she decided to join the fight, and charged straight toward the likely origin point of the shots. He bellowed a ragged cry, then deliberately tossed himself into a leaping roll toward another tree, closer to his target, and narrowly avoided another round.

As he tumbled into cover, it occurred to him that the rifleman probably wasn't one of the Ghost-Makers' very best. He had definite skill, but he seemed impatient and overly willing to prod his prey with testing shots or try to overwhelm them with fire. The highest echelon of snipers were those who rarely or never squeezed the trigger unless they were sure that death would result.

Ty sprang out of the roll, coming up on his feet behind the second tree, and sprayed another burst into the jungle, seven or eight rounds. Then he flipped the switch to semiauto as he charged up the slope, bobbing and weaving, firing the occasional single shot in his opponent's general direction.

The landscape was taking shape and becoming sensible again. The slope crested at a sort of tree line-ridge where several smaller trees grew in clusters that would've provided good places to hide, with a nice view of both sides of the hilltop. The sniper was surely somewhere up there.

Ty was about to spray the tree line with another volley of bullets when three shots rang out in perfectly spaced succession. They came not from the ridge but the lower region behind him and to the left, from the bush behind the big tree. Amahle had shot back.

Branches and leaves along the ridge swished. Ty squinted. Amahle had fired at a point around three yards to the left of where he'd guessed the hidden shooter lay. It made sense now that he looked closer. There was a small hollow there surrounded by light yet dense foliage.

Ty sprang out again, half-aiming as he blasted a round toward the hollow, then dove behind a tree once more.

This time, the sniper didn't shoot back.

He repeated his advance, and again, no one fired at him. His teeth clenched. Idiotic though it was, the frustration was coming back. He'd mentally prepared himself to storm the whole jungle if need be, cutting it down with his sword if he ran out of ammunition, only for Amahle to seemingly neutralize the threat when he'd least expected it.

As he moved closer, he heard a scream of pain. It wasn't connected to any further gunfire from his new partner. The sniper must have been hit, kept his mouth shut initially, and been unable to endure the anguish after he tried to move.

Ty's charge became more of a stalk as he cleared the rest of the distance. The fight seemed to be over. Still, a wounded man could be a dangerous one.

He kept his gun ready as he approached the spot from where the scream had come. Behind him, he faintly heard Amahle sliding up the ridge. She was hurrying, and therefore being less cautious than usual. Had she been taking her time, he might not have heard her at all.

Ty reached out and pushed aside a thick, leafy branch. It had a few vines and creepers attached, transforming it into a heavy green curtain. What he saw in the dark little hollow beyond didn't exactly shock or surprise him. It was still a dreadful, pitiful sight.

Lying there in the mud was a thin young man of below-average height, probably in his middle or late twenties. He had a gaunt, bony face, with dark curly hair and dark eyes which looked huge as they bulged from his skull. His skin was taut with the tension of pain and fear, but he hadn't yet seen or noticed Ty's presence.

One of his hands lay clamped over a bloody hole in his chest, where his left lung would be. That explained the gurgling way he kept gasping as he struggled for breath.

He'd dropped his scoped FN FAL rifle to lay against a root beside him. Not in his grasp, but easily within arm's reach.

Ty moved fast. He sprang into the hollow, and his foot lashed out, stomping down on the rifle and shoving it aside in one swift motion. The wounded young man noticed him at the same time, and his hand clawed for the weapon, missing it by an inch. When he failed, he leaned back, allowing his head to drop backward and his mouth to fall open in a sobbing groan while his eyes drew shut.

He knew the game was over, then, and that he'd lost.

Ty hesitated a second, his rifle aimed at the sniper but his finger off the trigger, while he tried to decide what to do. It might've been smart to finish the man off at once, removing even the remotest possibility that he might still pose a threat. Still, something about his pathetic despair suggested that he wasn't about to try anything and had resigned himself to death.

As such, questioning him might be a better idea. Before Ty could open his mouth, there was a faint rustling off to the side. Amahle burst through the foliage beside him, looking down at their mutual fallen adversary.

Amahle shook her head and muttered something under her breath. It sounded like a curse in whatever her native language was, combined with one or two random words in English. She, too, had her rifle ready but seemed in no hurry to deliver the coup de grace.

The wounded man looked up at Amahle. His eyes were still open about as wide as was physically possible, but otherwise, his face had an odd calm to it. He stared back at her in silence, aside from his panting gasps of pain.

Ty turned his eyes sidelong toward her while keeping his face pointed at the sniper in case he tried to draw a sidearm or something. "Do you know this guy? Is he one of the Ghost-Makers?"

Amahle nodded. "Yes, he is. They're in this jungle. If one of them is here, so are many others. They must be setting up a net in which to snare us. Or, perhaps, to snare the brother and sister. It's possible we merely became targets of opportunity."

"Great," Ty remarked. "How many more are there? Or, how many do they usually deploy for missions like this?"

He turned his eyes back to the man on the ground, who was once more staring at him with an unpleasant, focused resentment, as though he were mentally laying a curse upon those who'd mortally injured him.

Amahle responded, "I do not know. Only our leader would have that kind of information. She did not tell us everything so we couldn't divulge important things if anyone captured us.

"What I can tell you is this—everyone in our organization tended to work in fire teams of three. On any given assignment, there might be between one and five such teams. Five is the most I've ever seen. But it's always different, depending on the needs of the job. I worked with this man once and saw him with other teams several times."

"Okay, makes sense. So does that mean there are no more than fifteen Ghost-Makers total? Or are you guys more like a platoon-sized outfit? I can't imagine an elite sniper crew, especially one I've never heard of, being much bigger than that."

Amahle's tone carried a faint note of annoyance. "Again, I'm not sure. I believe there were about twenty or twenty-five of us at the time I left, but we sometimes lost people, and our leader would recruit new shooters to replace them without telling us."

Like most military units, then, they weren't a democracy. Ty decided to dismiss the issue for now. Based on what she'd divulged, there had probably been three snipers back at the valley, and there were probably two to five more in the jungle around them now.

Ty started to draw his pistol.

Amahle looked at him and held up a hand. "Wait. I would like to speak to him. He is young, and I used to work with him... I wish to ease his pain. I also want to see if I can find out anything from him that might be useful to us. We must know who is coordinating the Ghost-Makers since our leader was wounded by the sabotaged gun and falling from the heights of that tree."

"Sure," Ty quipped, "sounds good. But let's not take too long.

If your former partners always worked in three-person teams, the other two have to be out there somewhere. Either they're gunning for us directly, or they'll probably notice us on our way to the lodge. Especially after all that shooting."

Amahle waved as though she wasn't overly concerned. "Our standard protocol was always for team members to clear out and establish new positions, to maintain the net farther back. It's possible that with our leader gone, they will break protocol and do as they please."

Ty nodded. "I'll stand guard." He hoisted his rifle and stepped out to the edge of the screen of foliage surrounding the little hollow, his eyes scanning the jungle and the hills as the South African moved closer to interrogate the dying man. The wilderness was quiet again, apart from the ambient sounds of nature and its denizens. Yet even those seemed hushed after the roaring battle that had taken place minutes ago.

Behind him, Amahle knelt beside her wounded former coworker. She unslung a canteen of water and took a small white pill from her pack, probably an aspirin, and offered them to the young fellow. He pretended to ignore her at first, like a pouting and angry child trying not to acknowledge his parents, but after a moment of the woman's urging, he softened and accepted the pill along with a drink of water.

Ty glanced back and noticed the man's demeanor softening a little. The water alone probably made him feel a lot better, and the pill might help too—if he lived long enough for it to take effect.

Then, to Ty's surprise, Amahle moved close enough to put her arm around his shoulders and guide his head toward her lap, cradling him there. She took a clean cloth from a pouch and dampened it with water from the canteen, tenderly stroking the man's brow and cheek. When she spoke to him, it was in a gentle, conciliatory voice.

"Ibrahim," she began, "I'm sorry that things worked out this way, but..."

Her voice nearly trailed off as she practically whispered in his ear. Ty tried to listen, but he couldn't have heard most of it unless he stood brushing against her and leaned over them both. Doing so would've breached trust and left them open to attack. He would have to have faith that she would report all pertinent information to him after the fact.

Still, based on the words, phrases, and overall tone and timbre that he *could* discern, it sounded like Amahle was explaining her motivations, trying to console the young man, and beginning to ask questions. Ty wasn't sure if she was using English the whole time or switching to another tongue. The man had to speak at least some English or she wouldn't have bothered opening her statements to him with it, though.

Ty slowly circled the hollow. It was only perhaps eight or ten feet across, so it wasn't much of a patrol, and the movement might've drawn fire if any other snipers had scopes on them.

He wanted to get a good look at everything around them. Mostly there was endless dense foliage, with the slopes of the hills peeking through in places. There were no other sounds save those of birds and insects.

At no point did he hear Ibrahim respond to anything Amahle said. At least, not until he returned to his original point and looked at the pair. They almost resembled a mother and child at first glance. At times, Amahle didn't appear to be speaking to him at all but simply humming a song.

The man called Ibrahim was softening. He knew his life was over, that there was no recovery from his injury without a full hospital staff and modern equipment to treat him. That knowledge had made him slowly more accommodating of any final scraps of kindness and warmth he could attain before the end came.

Still, when Amahle urged him to "Tell me," he first shook his head.

Ty glanced around. He was reasonably confident that no one was about to take a potshot at them, so he slipped back into the hollow, drawing closer to the pair who clutched each other in the dark nest-like space.

Ibrahim tilted his face up and whispered something. Amahle blinked, then leaned closer.

She had no way of seeing what was about to happen, but Ty did. A faint stirring of motion—the man's hand remained clamped over his chest wound, but the other was moving at his belt. Ty saw the faintest glint of steel as Ibrahim drew a knife, intending to drag Amahle with him to the afterlife.

There was no time to shout a warning or attempt a complex and potentially dangerous disarming maneuver. There was time for nothing except an immediate and decisive strike. Ty leapt into action, his heart rate instantly tripling as his wakizashi flashed from its scabbard and he pushed forth, swinging.

Ibrahim cried out as the short sword's blade whizzed past him and his hand, clutching the knife, separated from his wrist in a shower of blood. Before it could strike the ground, Amahle snarled and pounced up and back, swinging her rifle up from its sling into a firing stance and taking a bead on Ty. The tip of his sword had come to a stop only a hand's length from her face.

Both froze. Ty kept his head still but flicked his eyes down and aside. Amahle did the same. Her expression, one of a ferocious animal about to defend itself, turned to one of dismayed understanding. Ibrahim's severed hand still clutched the short blade.

She exhaled through flaring nostrils, lowered her gun, and turned to her repudiated coworker with a frown of deep sadness and a slow headshake.

Ibrahim was trembling in pain and going pale, his body twitching. Ty had severed the main veins and arteries in his wrist, and he'd lost a fair amount of blood already from his chest wound. The shock of Ty's attack had sent him into convulsions that only made the hole in his lung worse. He would be dead in less than a minute, Ty guessed.

The young man didn't share Amahle's somber mood. He was determined to go out with defiance.

Grimacing and spitting at her with what little life he had remaining, he hissed, "She-Wolf is coming for you."

CHAPTER ELEVEN

Tyler and Amahle stood, tense and unspeaking, as Ibrahim finally let out a long, croaking gasp and slumped against the ground. His eyes rolled back and turned dull, and he lay perfectly still.

Ty turned to his partner. "Who is She-Wolf?" He could guess, but he didn't want to say it aloud.

Amahle didn't respond right away. She stared at the young man's corpse, and the expression on her face was something new. Ibrahim's ugly end had already made her morose, it seemed, but now her mouth puckered while her shoulders rose a notch or two. She almost seemed faintly...ashamed?

And afraid. The young marksman's final words had chilled her.

That all but confirmed Ty's lurking suspicion. She-Wolf was the Ghost-Makers' leader—and she was still alive. The rounds fired at her, the booby-trapped gun, and the tumble from the tree hadn't killed the woman who was now Amahle's deadly enemy.

The South African drew a deep breath and half-turned toward him, but her eyes remained downcast in her vague embarrassment. "You saved my life. My thanks for that, Tyler Katakura."

"You're welcome." He spoke in a neutral but courteous tone. Americanized and cynical as he was, the traditional Japanese concern for politeness and decorum had never entirely abandoned him. "Don't mention it."

He realized, after a second, that he was speaking to himself in a way since it might be best not to mention his other conclusion. Amahle was mentally beating herself up over her failure to eliminate her former boss. Now She-Wolf would undoubtedly want revenge in addition to needing to complete the Ghost-Makers' mission to earn their pay.

If he put Amahle on the spot—if he pressed her too hard on the issue and potentially made her feel as though she'd made a terrible mistake—it might impugn her effectiveness in scouting and combat. With the odds arrayed against them, the two of them would need to operate at the height of their abilities.

He swept aside the growing miasma of discomfort by trying to get her to focus on practical things. "We should get moving again. With all that shooting, if Hugh and Tilda are nearby, they probably got wind of it. I wouldn't be surprised if they're picking up the pace and getting itchy. They might get away. Or they might do something stupid."

His hands twisted tightly around the grip and barrel shroud of his rifle. He almost wished he hadn't said *that*. The thought of the Ashcroft twins doing something to Daria in their impatience was nearly enough to impact *his* effectiveness.

"Yes," Amahle agreed. "Come, let us go. Stay close to me. We must move faster than we had before. We need not worry so much about being quiet. Everyone nearby knows that we're here."

She shook her head one final time to clear her mind of dark thoughts, then hitched her rifle over her shoulder and strode out of the hollow to stand upon the ridge's peak.

Ty sprang out, annoyed that she'd outpaced him the instant she started walking. His mind rapidly regained what it had learned about moving in the same style she used. Without the necessity for stealth and near-total silence, it was easier to keep up, anyway. He tried to avoid breaking sticks beneath his boots or swishing through too many leaves.

Still, it was a relief to be able to barrel through or vault over things. There was no time to blend into the landscape itself.

The mists were thinning a little. It was now well into the afternoon, and the day was warm and relatively sunny. Little light penetrated to the jungle's floor, but there was still enough solar energy to disperse the worst of the fog. Ty could see more and gain a better understanding of his surroundings.

Most notably, he saw that things looked familiar. They weren't far from the lodge. He was pretty sure that it lay on the terrace-ridge beyond the next hill in front of them.

Ty stuck close to Amahle as she led the way. He was able to keep within about two yards of her, sometimes closer to one yard, depending on the terrain.

Past the crest of the ridge, there was a broad, relatively shallow valley. Its bottom was still significantly higher than the base of the first hill they'd climbed. Beyond it was another, smaller hillock, then the terraced mountainside that was their likely target.

They had a workout ahead of them. Going downhill was a relief, but it would be short-lived.

As they ascended the next slope, it occurred to Ty that they were potentially sitting ducks if Ibrahim's comrades were anywhere in the woods above them. Yet Amahle was experienced enough that she must've considered the possibility.

Ty drew closer to her. There was a kind of silent warmth emanating from her, a faint appreciation for what he'd done. She *knew* that he was sparing her the shame and guilt of having to discuss the She-Wolf situation. She was grateful for it.

Still, as to their current situation, there was at least one question that required an answer.

"How do we know that they're not taking a bead on us right now? Or that we won't stumble into another ambush?" he inquired in a soft voice during one of the brief lulls in their relentless drive forward.

The question didn't faze Amahle. If anything, she probably appreciated the good sense he showed in wondering about it.

"The net might be shifting in response to what has occurred," she declared, meaning Ibrahim's loss. "It's highly unlikely that they will pursue us or that they're close enough to shoot at us from here. The net tactic is more about containment. It is to stop the quarry, not hound them down. If we continue to move quickly while we're inside the perimeter, they won't catch us again."

Ty nodded. Sniper stuff wasn't his specialty in military maneuvers, but it made sense. Something else occurred to him, though. "What about when we're ready to move *outside* the perimeter?"

Amahle let out a barely audible sigh, but her attention remained focused on the land around her. Her dark eyes searched the jungle to be safe. "Getting out will be much more difficult, yes. The others in Ibrahim's fire team will have constricted around us and perhaps joined the other team if there is a second. There might be. I don't know."

Ty had suspected that the proverbial other shoe might drop. He grimaced, putting all thought of their escape out of his head for the time being. "Let's find Daria first. One batch of reckless heroics at a time, if you please. The human brain isn't supposed to think about death-defying stupidity all goddamn day."

The woman shot him an odd, squinty look, then her mouth creased in a half-smile. She let out a brief, sharp laugh. "Ha. The Western sarcasm. I'm still growing familiar with it. Your idea is a good one. We cannot do everything at once."

As they loped along, gaining their second wind midway up the second hill, Ty reflected on the fact that she thought of him as a Westerner. He *was* an American, after all, and he talked like one despite everything.

In America itself, as soon as he ventured outside the small *nisei* community, no one ever allowed him to forget that he was Japanese. In a place like Atlantica, where the population was an utter jumble of new arrivals and no group was more dominant than any other, everyone seemed to think of him as simply a former U.S. soldier from California.

Which he was.

The pair were growing winded by the time they reached the final ascent. Ty recognized the lay of the land. The chateau's outer grounds would be within sight in a matter of minutes if all went well. He was impressed with himself and his new compatriot for covering so much ground so quickly.

Amahle shot him approving glances here and there as well. Both were vigorously athletic despite not being as young as they once were. Despite the different nature of their experiences, neither had been anything but a warrior since adolescence.

Ty's competitive streak reasserted itself. He had, after all, been on this mountainside before, and he wanted to prove that he could scale it even more efficiently this time than he had a day ago. It would be amusing to beat Amahle at her game.

Not that he wanted to humiliate her or anything like that. Nor did he feel much threatened by her. It would simply be fun.

The South African cryptically perceived his intention and picked up her pace as he threatened to pull ahead. She must've been the type of child who'd challenged her friends to a race every time they went anywhere.

They were halfway up the ridge when it became obvious that neither would leave the other in the dust. Both slowed their climb a little.

Then they stopped after cresting a boulder that overlooked the gentlest part of the hill. The chateau's peaked roof was in sight, past the edge of the terrace and the tops of the surrounding trees.

In a gentle whisper, Ty asked, "Okay, how do we make our approach? Over there is the easiest path. If they're expecting us, it's the first place they'd post a guard." He gestured at a shallow gully on the edge of the jungle not far from the outer gate within the lodge's bullet hole-riddled outer wall.

Amahle raised a hand. "Give me a moment. So far, we cannot hear anything. We might be the first to arrive here."

Ty nodded. That would be the best-case scenario. If indeed they'd beaten the Ghost-Makers to the prize, the two of them could pick the turf they fought on. Ty could provide a brief distraction while Amahle put a bullet in Hugh's and Tilda's heads before either knew what was going on and Daria would be safe.

Bitter experience had taught him, though, that best-case scenarios were rarely the way things turned out.

Something else popped into his head. He turned his eyes toward Amahle's. "How well do you know your old team?"

The woman shook her head. "I don't think they're moving in on the lodge yet. Unless you've seen or heard something that I have not."

"No, that's not what I meant. I mean, were you close to them?" He paused as his meaning sank in. "With Ibrahim back there, well...the way you acted with him, it was like he was a friend, or a little brother or something. I thought maybe you two...you know, cared about each other. Before things went sour."

Asking such a thing was perhaps a bad idea, Ty considered. She might not have wanted to talk about it. He couldn't get the image of her cradling the young man's head out of his mind, and the way Ibrahim's angry attempt to kill her had possessed the distinctive sting of personal betrayal.

Amahle let out a slow, gentle sigh, only distinguishable from a normal exhalation by the faint hum that accompanied it. She was trying to think of a response.

Ty decided to clarify his intentions.

"I mainly ask because I want your head in the game. I can tell it bothered you, that you didn't want to see him die like that. It's okay to be sorry it happened. But if we're going to get through this, neither of us can be preoccupied with personal stuff." He tried to keep his tone sympathetic. The words themselves were already on the harsh side.

Amahle cleared her throat. "I understand. Please, give me a moment."

"Okay." He looked up at the lodge. "I'm concerned. You might even say I feel bad about the whole thing. I served in the war in Korea when the Chinese helped the Communists in the north invade, and the U.S. went over to help stop them. Maybe it was worth it. Maybe it wasn't. I lost some brothers in arms. Good men whom I cared about. It can be hard. I know how it is."

Amahle closed her eyes. "I didn't only *know* Ibrahim, Mr. Katakura. I also helped to train him when he first became a member of the Ghost-Makers. I was a squad leader. He was my responsibility, and he reminded me of myself when I was a little younger. Like me, he was a person with a gift for violence who was tired of being used by those who are powerful and ruthless."

Ty wondered where the young man had come from. He guessed one of the Arab countries, but it was difficult to be sure.

The woman continued, "He believed, much as I used to, that carrying a rifle for the Ghost-Makers outfit was a way to have the freedom to *use* that gift for violence. To make good with it, free from the manipulations and conceits of the warlords, politicians, and business people. However, it seems that anywhere wealth and power begin to take root, they grow into a deadly plant that chokes and poisons everything. Even in a place such as Atlantica, so anarchic and untamed. Perhaps it is only human nature, and there was never... Maybe..."

Ty could tell that she was struggling, that she wanted to say more and admit to a litany of self-doubts and second thoughts, to confess how often she'd skated along the brink of despair. She was too proud to break down in front of someone else in such a fashion. Certainly not someone she'd known for mere hours.

He had to respect that. He bobbed his head twice to acknowledge all she chose to leave unsaid.

"We can't stop people from being people," he conceded, his voice gruff but not unkind. "As cruel, stupid, and shortsighted as they sometimes tend to be. We can set standards and try to reward the good. When some of them cross the line, someone must be there to hold them accountable. That's what it means to be an Executioner."

Amahle looked at him full in the face, now, and her scarred features had become lovely with the dropping of her guard. It was amazing how well they'd come to know each other and how things had evolved between them over less than half a day.

Being in deadly combat had a way of forging ties that stayed stronger than those formed in peace. And—

An engine whined. Somewhere in the distance, yet not too far away. Up at the chateau.

Amahle cast her eyes in that direction and tensed, falling automatically into a defensive crouch with her rifle shouldered. "What is that?"

It took Ty a second or two to recognize the noise. Something he recalled from his later military days, an unpleasant sound in and of itself, but one that sometimes meant aid and rescue. Hearing it now could only mean bad things.

It meant he should've spent an extra half a minute scouting out the lodge when he was there before, sniper fire or no. It meant that they were too late.

"Are you *fucking* kidding me?" he exclaimed.

It was the sound of a Bell H-13 Sioux helicopter, firing up and ready to take off.

CHAPTER TWELVE

"Go!" Ty shouted, waving Amahle forward an instant before he plunged into the gully himself.

She jumped onto the upper-left edge of the channel, rifle up and ready, her feet nimbly finding purchase on the uneven ground while she weaved to and fro, ducking under branches. There was no time for subtlety, finesse, or secretiveness. There was only the absolute necessity of haste.

Ty did much the same. With his slightly larger frame and longer legs, his stomping run allowed him to plow through the mud in the gully and bull his way past the branches that hung across it or break through any vines.

They were still moving uphill. The distance was short. In fact, under the light of day and with the need for stealth removed, it seemed much, much shorter than it had last night when Ty had crept slowly through the last of the jungle before infiltrating the estate proper.

The helicopter's distinctive noise was louder when the pair burst free of the foliage and into the yard. That meant the blades had begun spinning in addition to the engine running. It would be ready for takeoff at any moment.

Ty's lungs heaved, and his mouth hung open. With his voice loud and ragged, he bellowed, "That way! Behind the shed."

It was the only place on the property he could think of where the hunters' cult would've been able to hide a goddamn helipad from easy sight. The sounds seemed to be coming from there.

Much to his dismay and embarrassment, though, it also meant that he'd been practically on top of the thing when he'd charged the Ashcroft siblings as they mounted their armored personnel carrier.

In the brief space of time he possessed before his total focus shifted to action, he cursed and lamented the Ghost-Makers for driving him to such haste. Without snipers firing on him last night, he would've had time to search the whole property and make a proper account of things.

Amahle wove around behind Ty and circled toward the back of the chateau outside the surrounding wall. Ty was about to yell at her to follow him, but he stopped himself. God forbid, if the helicopter were able to take off before he could get to it, she would be in a better position to see where it headed.

Ty kept inside the wall. That was where the APC's garage had been. As the outbuilding came into sight, he moved left, closer to the lodge proper, ignoring and running over the debris from the shattered windows and blasted walls from the night's carnage.

Halfway to the shed, his stomach churned, and his heart sank. An oval blur appeared behind the building, rising, and below it the distinctive insect-like shape of the H-13. He couldn't see much in the cockpit, but all three of the airborne vessel's seats appeared to have occupants.

"No!" he barked, trying to sprint the rest of the way to the helipad, but he knew it was useless. "No, goddammit!" Even if he could clamber atop the garage and jump for the helicopter's bottom rung, there wouldn't be enough time to get to it.

By the time he reached the edge of the shed, the chopper had cleared the encircling wall and swung over the treetops of the surrounding jungle. Hugh and Tilda had escaped with Daria in tow.

Ty ran over the helipad, wanting to spit on it although it would be useless and would rob him of precious time and equally precious moisture. He made a beeline for the nearest exit gap in the wall, shouting, "Amahle! Don't shoot. Daria is aboard that thing."

As he came to an exit and emerged into the estate's brief surrounding yard area, it was clear that something aboard the Sioux wasn't right.

It had begun to wobble and shake in midair, not traversing much distance as it struggled simply to remain in the sky, as though whoever was at the controls were having a serious personal or medical problem. Ty ran toward the jungle's edge, noting Amahle's silhouette out of the corner of his eye, approaching from his right.

He saw—faintly—a violent blur of motion within the helicopter's cockpit. A struggle had broken out among the occupants. It was impossible to make out faces or details. All he could tell for sure was that things weren't going according to the Ashcrofts' plans.

Ty shouldered his rifle and stopped where he was. Powerful though it was, his AR-10 was highly unlikely to be able to bring a chopper down, even if it dipped low enough that there was a chance Daria might survive the crash. He watched in horror.

Once again, he was helpless. Things were going wrong in front of his eyes, and there was virtually nothing he could do.

The H-13 lurched, wavering up and down like a drunk struggling to keep its balance and inscribing circles above the tree line. It was only about fifty yards from where Ty stood. Since the troubles within the cockpit had begun, it had barely moved away from the lodge.

Amahle came up beside Ty. In a hushed yet hurried voice, she asserted, "We might be able to shoot it down if we aim for the back. The trees would soften the fall. But there is much risk."

Trying to swallow with his throat suddenly dry, Tyler gulped. "No. We can't chance it. I don't know what to do."

His only option was to trust Daria, to have faith that she might, against all odds, overpower her captors and seize control of the chopper to bring it to a safe landing.

Then, readily visible behind the helicopter's windshield even in the glare of the sun, came the muzzle flare of a gun. The air cracked loudly with the report at the same moment.

Ty stomped in frustration. He trotted toward the jungle as the Sioux finally started on a straight course down the jumble of hills toward the lowlands. It was banking hard to one side, like a driverless car with something weighted against its gas pedal. Ty didn't want to lose sight of it, but letting it get too far away wouldn't be much better.

The chopper dipped and rose again. At the lowest point of its temporary descent, someone fell out the side.

Amahle exclaimed something in her native tongue. Ty could only stare, transfixed, attempting to reject the information being foisted onto his brain by reality.

The helicopter had buzzed too far off to confirm many details, but the person who'd tumbled out of the cockpit appeared to be slim with long dark hair. The scream of terror that resounded over the forest was higher-pitched and distinctly feminine.

Then Ty barged straight into the woods, headed toward the spot where the passenger had fallen. He bludgeoned the foliage out of the way with his shoulder, knocked it aside with his rifle butt, or stomped on it with his boots. Nothing would deter him from reaching the site.

He was dimly aware of Amahle plunging into the fray behind him. For once, she struggled to keep up with him rather than the reverse.

Ty dimly realized in the rear corner of his mind still devoted to rational thought, that he'd finally transcended the limitations imposed on him all day by his emotional reactions to so much bad luck. He was truly back in warrior mode—*zanshin* and *mushin*, the states of no-mind, of total awareness without conscious abstract thought.

Huge roots, python-like, rose out of the ground before him, sometimes revealing themselves with bare fractions of a second before he tripped over them, possibly breaking his leg in the process. He smoothly leapt over them and hit the ground running.

Claw-like branches reached out to snare him in nets of ivy and creepers. Without breaking stride, he swatted them away or clove them in two with his sword.

As the foliage grew denser, he hung his rifle over his shoulder and kept the wakizashi out instead. A fine sword with a fine edge wasn't the ideal tool to use against crude jungle vegetation, but he could repair the edge later. He didn't have a machete.

With the sky becoming visible as he and Amahle streaked through a relatively barren patch of earth, they saw the helicopter. It shuddered and spewed smoke from its engine a second before the report of two or three rifle shots, virtually simultaneous, echoed across the forest.

Then the H-13 stopped even trying to fly. Its propellers slowed, and it sank into the trees while still hurtling forward at high speed. The terrible clamor of splintering wood and shrieking, distorted metal rose from the site of its crash landing.

Ty's new state of focus threatened to dissipate. If Daria wasn't the one who'd fallen out of the chopper mid-flight, she'd been on the vehicle as it plunged to its destruction.

He refused to think about it, any of it. The only thing that mattered was getting there and seeing for himself. He could decide how to interpret the evidence later.

Amahle patted his shoulder while keeping up a jog beside

him. "If we go that way and bear to the left, we'll cross the point where the woman fell while still being on the way to where the helicopter went down."

"Yeah," Ty grunted. "Good."

His partner had more to say, though. "We can expect that the Ghost-Makers will be closing in on the crash. There will be heavy overwatch. We must be fast and lucky, or we will have their rifles on us."

Ty's blood was up. The rage was still there, but now it was subject to his resurgence of discipline. It made him feel...confident.

"Let them try to stop me," he huffed, then plunged into the brush. Amahle was right there beside him.

Here the ground ran downhill a little more steeply, not enough to make it overly treacherous, but enough that gravity was on their side as they picked up speed. The plant life was also somewhat less dense.

As they got closer to their first of two destinations, Ty saw a stream winding through the forest and partially breaking up the clusters of trees. It appeared to broaden in the shallow valley down below. There was also a small clearing off to the side where the woman—whoever she was—had plummeted.

Despite not having to fight their way uphill, Ty and Amahle were huffing and drenched with sweat when they reached the slope's bottom, at the beginning of the flat valley. To the best of Ty's memory, the passenger had tumbled out of the chopper near the clearing's right-hand edge. She must've been somewhere within the first ten or twenty yards of the tree line.

Ty caught Amahle's gaze and gestured with his chin toward the closer but denser part of the jungle, then stepped toward the more distal but less vine-choked portion a little farther away for himself to search. The woman nodded and slipped into the trees.

After a short jog across the clearing's edge, Ty figured he was far enough that his and Amahle's search areas wouldn't overlap while keeping them close enough that they could easily communicate and regroup if need be.

He ducked under a branch and entered the jungle as the air above him exploded.

The shockwave rippled his skin and rattled his bones and teeth. The sound was like that of the inner pressure of an artillery shell being fired, complete with the same disturbance in the air pressure and sense of impending doom. He threw himself to the ground and prayed that Amahle had the sense to do the same.

Yet there came no boom, as would be expected with a large explosive shell. Instead, there was a strange beat of silence and a sharp *crack*, loud but not deafening—and not rifle fire.

Trees around him splintered and toppled, their trunks blasted to wood chips, and the creaking groans filled the rainforest's thick air. Cursing silently, he ducked, rolled, sprang up, and ran to avoid two trees that might've crushed him otherwise. Around the woods, others fell in a similar fashion.

He looked across from him. Amahle was there, having narrowly escaped the devastation herself. The intense look of quizzical alarm on her dark face suggested that she was as baffled as he was. They waited together a moment, neither speaking nor breathing.

When nothing happened, both examined their surroundings. The trees had been cut down in a line, slightly jagged and irregular like a bolt of lightning. It stretched from twenty or thirty yards behind them, through the jungle toward the plume of smoke that must've been the helicopter crash site and beyond.

Ty's mouth fell open. "What could've done this?" he breathed.

"If I am honest," Amahle said, "I was going to ask you that same question."

Rifles thundering broke the silence, at least two or three of them trading shots somewhere up ahead. Another weird pulse followed the blasts, which they *felt* as much as heard—and, once again, a strange cracking of the air that came from no mere firearm Ty had ever heard of. It was farther away this time.

He and Amahle ducked to the ground, watching the trees around them. None splintered or fell.

The pair exchanged glances. Neither wanted to admit that they were frightened and had no idea what to do but recognized that each probably felt the same way. In the quiet that gradually set in, they tried to think.

Then, from somewhere above them, they heard hacking and a choked peal of laughter. Concurrently with the disturbing sound, drops of bright red liquid rained down onto the ground in front of them and off to the right.

Both Ty and Amahle slowly looked up. They had a pretty good idea of what to expect. Still, neither looked forward to seeing it.

At about a two o'clock position to them and perhaps twelve to fifteen feet off the ground, the mangled but still-living body of Tilda Ashcroft hung amid a giant pincushion of tree branches. Some of them were dead and bare as skeletal fingers aside from the sheets of dull green moss that clung to the half-rotten trunk. Her limbs and torso were unpleasantly contorted, her head rested askew on one shoulder, and some of the sharper tips of the stouter branches emerged slick with crimson from her back. They'd skewered her through the stomach and inner shoulder.

Ty grimaced at the awful sight. It couldn't have happened to a more deserving person, but it was still gruesome to behold. Snapped-off vines dangled over the woman's body as well. The waning afternoon sun backlit her where it shone freely through a patch of obliterated vegetation where Tilda had initially crashed through the canopy.

Technically, the mission of executing her was still on the table. Given the nature of her injuries and the large amount of blood she'd lost, anything Ty or Amahle could do would be a moot and redundant point.

Tilda's blue eyes, bright and crazed, caught sight of them, and her mouth opened in a crooked smile, revealing blood-flecked teeth.

"Hugh..." she gasped. "He never could keep it...in his pants." She giggled, then choked and spat up more blood. "He had to...get it off, at least a little, one last time before...the end."

Ty felt his gorge rising, and with it, his anger. He raised his rifle. "All right, unless you tell us what we want to know, you're—"

Amahle's hand was suddenly on his arm with a gentle but firm touch. Then she pushed the gun's barrel down. He squinted with annoyance but let her.

The South African called up to the dying woman, using a gentle tone not unlike that she'd employed with Ibrahim, though louder to account for the added distance. "Tilda. I will put you out of your misery. We know it is over, and I'm sure you want it to end soon. But please, you must tell us what caused this devastation around us."

Tilda laughed, but her body convulsed in pain when she did. Her once-beautiful face took on a sneer made worse by her grayish skin tone now that she'd lost half or more of her blood.

Then she looked at Ty, speaking to him instead of Amahle. "You think we're monsters, but you haven't seen...the real monsters." Blood dribbled from the corner of her mouth. "My brother and I... Sure, we killed a few people here and there. The Coven...they're going to take over the world or burn it down trying."

"Maybe," Ty said in a flat tone. "Maybe not." He rose to his feet and turned away. Amahle could do what she wanted, but he had no desire to do anything except leave Tilda there until nature ran its course. "Either way, you'll be in Hell long before the rest of us. You and your brother."

He walked away into the clearing and toward the helicopter's crash site. A moment later, a rifle *cracked* once.

Looking back, he saw Amahle striding toward him with her gun over her shoulder. Her face was blank of any particular expression. Behind her, Tilda hung silent and motionless in the tree.

Once the woman was by his side, they both strode off into the jungle.

Ty opined, "Better than she deserved. Do you know the sort of sick shit those two did?"

"I do not need to know what they did or how this started." Amahle kept pace beside him. "I only know that I finish things."

CHAPTER THIRTEEN

Ty briefly allowed himself the satisfaction of knowing that Tilda, the hunter of humans, would now find her earthly remains devoured by scavengers who didn't discriminate between species. It was a grim and vicious thought, but he'd been having a rather bad day. Knowing the world was rid of at least one of the Ashcroft siblings represented a silver lining of sorts.

There was another upside to the situation that was of immediate pragmatic value.

The bizarre destructive effect they'd witnessed minutes ago had cleared a straight path through the jungle for them. It led more or less directly to the site of the crashed H-13 Sioux. Smoke still rose from the chopper's wreckage, providing an easy beacon. Getting there would be faster with half of the trees and vegetation blasted into little more than a mulch carpet.

Ty jogged along the unnatural path. Amahle's incredible skill at navigating dense wilderness served her well in the rainforest and on hillsides, but they were now moving through a relatively flat corridor. Thus, Ty's longer legs allowed him to pull out in front.

To Amahle's credit, she was never far behind. Ty wouldn't

have wanted to get too far ahead, anyway. She deserved to be by his side through whatever was about to come at them. Plus, she was handy enough with a rifle that his chances of surviving through the next hour were far better with her there to oppose the other Ghost-Makers.

The blast path led them about half a mile toward a slightly more elevated, terrace-like area near the valley's edge. The terrain beyond it ascended into rambling foothills. They were most of the way there and could almost make out the helicopter's wreckage when the gunshots started anew.

"God*dammit*," Ty muttered. He kept his head down, but nothing suggested that the rifles were firing at him. If the Ghost-Makers were shooting at the downed chopper, someone must've still been alive. However, their chances of living much longer were far from good.

Ty picked up the pace, his fast jog becoming an all-out sprint despite the dangers ahead and regardless of how tired he was growing after the day's heavy exertions. Without slowing or breaking stride, he swung his AR-10 off his shoulder and caught it firmly in his hands. He was pretty damn sure he would need it momentarily.

Amahle lagged. As the distance between them expanded, Ty slowed and shuffled to a halt. The jungle ahead had opened, thanks to the combined devastation of the crash and the weird invisible weapon or whatever it was. For an instant, before either of them leapt into action, Ty and Amahle saw everything happening at the crash site.

The Bell H-13 Sioux wasn't a particularly robust chopper, consisting of little more than steel latticework, an engine housing, and a windshield. When it plunged into the forest, it had snagged on the trees and lacked the mass or energy to crush them out of the way. Part of its tail had wrapped around a stout trunk, and the remains of it still drooped from the branches like metal vines.

The cockpit had slammed into the damp, muddy earth near the stream that flowed through the valley. Small parts of the engine were scattered around along with shards of glass and twisted metal scraps, some of them burning amid the general wreckage and sending up plumes of black smoke.

Half-crouched behind what appeared to be the disembodied floor of the chopper's cockpit was Hugh Ashcroft. The effects of the tumble had neither killed nor crippled him, but he looked even more bloodied, battered, and ill-treated in general than he had after Ty had slashed him a couple of times.

Yet, he was *animated.* A crazy grin covered his face, the look of a man who'd stopped caring what happened and was determined to squeeze what enjoyment he could from objectively awful circumstances. His eyes were wide, bright, and bloodshot. In his hands was an M1 carbine loaded with a thirty-round magazine, and he kept poking it over the edge of the makeshift barricade to trade shots with his enemies.

Ty could barely glimpse the outlines and silhouettes of the figures farther out in the forest, with whom Hugh engaged in mortal combat.

They were wearing camouflage but not full ghillie suits by the looks of it, and they'd chosen their positions well—plenty of foliage concealment and an open line of fire. There were two that Ty could be sure of. Others might be hiding somewhere else. The pair he could see had positioned themselves at both points of a roughly ninety-degree angle that extended outward from the obliterated copter.

So far there was no sign of Daria. This meant that as far as Ty was concerned, no one in the glade in front of him was a friend. He refused to pick a side and would rather see them all dead.

He raised his rifle, aiming at Hugh, the nearest and most obvious target. Beside him, Amahle made a faint sighing or muttering sound, as though she were about to protest or try to reason with him but had changed her mind at the last instant.

The world narrowed to only what Tyler could see beyond the muzzle of his gun. The front sight hovered over Hugh's head, and the barrel's drift slowed and all but stopped as Ty exhaled, didn't breathe back in, and let a focused stillness settle over him.

The other Ashcroft, like his sister, would get better than he deserved. He wouldn't know what had hit him. His head would simply cease to exist. Then off he would go to whatever powers lay beyond this world. The Earth would no longer have to deal with him.

Ty's finger curled around the trigger as a second figure emerged from behind a fat fallen log, a woman holding and aiming a pistol. She popped off two shots in the same direction Hugh was firing. Her chest lay almost directly behind Hugh's head. Ty tensed, shuddered, and took his finger off the trigger.

Daria and Hugh were fighting *together*.

Amahle moved a step closer to Ty. In a low voice, she observed, "He seems quite quick to forget who threw his sister out of a helicopter twenty minutes ago."

Without further commentary, she brought her Remington 700 up to her shoulder and peered down the sights. Not at Daria or Hugh, but at the closer of the two camouflaged figures out in the bush.

Ty let his weapon fall to low ready as he squinted, taking in the whole scene and trying to assess what to do. He could open fire on the Ghost-Makers, but he didn't have a particularly clear shot. So he might accomplish nothing except draw premature attention to himself and his new partner.

Looking at Hugh, he murmured, "Maybe Tilda fell. The chopper was swerving all over the fucking place." He peered around for better vantage points, but the valley was almost flat. "Besides, it's amazing how forgiving you can become when someone starts shooting back at the same people who're shooting at you."

He recalled an incident back in Korea when a fellow G.I. with an excessively big mouth spouted off his opinions about the Japanese, based on his older brother's experiences in the previous war. He and Ty had been about a minute from trying to strangle one another. Then the Communists had attacked, and they forgot it. The man had saved Ty's life with a well-placed shot and nodded at him before hurrying off to another part of the skirmish line.

Amahle laughed softly. Ty hadn't intended his remark as a joke, but he would take what he could get.

Then the South African took careful aim at the jungle beyond the crash site. She had the advantage of a scope and was probably better suited than Ty for taking a lengthy shot at a partially obscured target.

Ty thought about sharing his concerns with her that they'd draw attention to themselves. Then he recalled her earlier coup de grace on Tilda. The combatants ahead of them must've known that *someone* was out in the woods besides themselves.

In a beat of silence between the back-and-forth gunplay nearer the stream, Amahle became as still as though she were a bronze sculpture. Then she cracked off a single shot.

A leaf somewhere far out in the forest drifted toward the ground, severed from its parent branch. A human cried out in pain and alarm.

Hugh and Daria glanced around in confusion. They couldn't see their rescuers yet and probably thought another sniper had appeared to finish them off. The time to intervene more directly was now.

Ty barked, "I'm going in to get Daria out. Cover me!" He brought his rifle up to his chest, sucked in his breath, and dashed forward, taking note of the potential cover spots along the way but otherwise intending to make a beeline for Executioner Barruk.

Amahle raised her voice. "What about Hugh?"

"Haven't decided yet," Ty called over his shoulder. He plowed ahead, thinking of virtually nothing except how best to extract his comrade while keeping her and himself alive. Killing their enemies could come later. Or, perhaps it would happen anyway as a side-effect of fulfilling his primary objective.

Two seconds into his charge, though, a heavy rifle round whizzed past him and ripped up the ground five feet behind him and to the rear. He was pretty sure it was a stray bullet or one meant for Amahle, but stray bullets didn't care who they killed. Keeping himself out of the line of fire was still an issue.

He darted aside, zigging and zagging as needed to take cover behind thick trees or below slight bumps and rises in the earth. Amahle was keeping watch behind him but hadn't yet fired again. The majority of the shooting was still between Hugh and Daria on one side and the assassins on the other.

As Ty drew closer to his target, another problem presented itself. One so obvious he cursed himself for not considering it sooner. The wrecked chopper, and by extension Daria, lay on the other side of the stream. With everything else going on, he hadn't stopped to consider that fording it might be more challenging than it had looked from a distance.

A stray bullet ripped past him, blasting a shower of splinters from a nearby tree. Ty ignored it. All his senses were alert to danger, but he was desensitized by now to the stress of gunfire.

A few feet ahead of him, the trees gave way to weeds, and the ground turned to pure mud beside the stream's lapping brownish waters. It was about four yards wide, he guessed, and he couldn't tell by looking at it how deep it was or how strong the current might be. Sucking in his breath and raising his rifle to hold it beneath his chin, he plunged in.

The water was colder than he expected, to the point of being bracing and setting his teeth to rattling. The current was weak at first. As he waded out a good five feet, the bottom dropped rapidly. Then the water's passage was strong enough that each step became a struggle not to get swept off his feet or pushed downstream. Also, rocks, roots, and other obstructions lay strewn across the stream bed.

Ty inhaled through his nose and exhaled through his mouth, keeping his mind calm although he wanted to rush through the latter half of the stream and get it over with. Everything was taking too long.

With Hugh so close, part of his mind kept telling him to aim his rifle and finish off the bastard. Still, firing into the battle would only draw extra attention to him. So far, the snipers either hadn't seen him or were deliberately saving him until after they'd dealt with the remaining Ashcroft. And Daria.

Behind him, he heard no gunshots coming from Amahle's rifle, and the rushing of water blocked out what minuscule amount of noise she might've made if she were advancing through the forest. He trusted her abilities, but they hadn't had time to coordinate their strategy for extracting Daria and getting out of Dodge.

He would have to assume that it was all up to him.

The stream's current took a sudden increase at the same time that the creek bed bottomed out by nearly a foot of extra depth. Ty stumbled forward, then sideways, as he lost his balance. The water was up to his chest. He let it carry him a short way, maybe ten feet, then struggled forward until the water was shallow enough for him to plant his feet again and crash through the rest of the current, emerging dripping on the opposite bank.

As he found his stance on dry ground and readied his rifle for action, he finally heard the voices of the pair hiding behind the helicopter's wreckage.

Daria, still apparently oblivious to Ty's presence, shouted, "We have to move!" Less than a second after she spoke, she ducked in time to evade a sudden burst of gunfire that riddled the ground, foliage, and water behind her with bullets.

Ty noted the close spacing of the shots. Another Ghost-Maker might've arrived and supported the others with a full auto weapon. Alternately, there might now be at least four or five of them and they were coordinating their shots into a barrage, hoping to overwhelm their foes with sheer firepower.

Despite this, Hugh scoffed and sneered at Daria's recommendation.

"You run, then!" He cackled madly, as though something had struck him as so funny that he was on the verge of falling over, and let his carbine drop to hang from his shoulder by its sling. "*I'm* going to teach these sons of bitches why you don't cross H&T!"

With a rapid and abrupt motion, he reached down with his right hand and came back up holding something that Ty immediately recognized as a weapon, but which nonetheless made him blink in total confusion.

It looked like something designed by a person who'd read too many science fiction comic books. The first thing Ty thought of when he saw it was one of the ray guns that always showed up in the hands of hostile Martians.

Daria glanced at him, and her expression distorted in alarm or anger. Ty had a sudden sinking feeling deep within his gut. He hastened up the shoreline, hoping that trying to intervene wouldn't get them all killed.

The ray gun, or whatever it was, had been put together rather crudely, to the point that Ty wondered if it was a homemade model or toy and Hugh's sanity had finally cracked apart altogether. A lower metal frame, possibly from an old Mauser C96, sprouted an array of jagged assemblies of steel and aluminum and a tubular barrel at the center, with entire spools' worth of copper wire wrapped around it in a chaotic vortex of spirals. It was difficult to tell if the wire held the whole mess together by mere friction or if it was a power source or otherwise served a more obscure function.

Ty's initial impression that the ridiculous thing might be a toy dispelled instantly. Somewhere within the center of the gun, a peculiar blue glow had begun to shine, growing in strength like someone kindling a fire.

Once, long ago, he might've tried to dismiss it as "a toy that has a blue light inside it." Now he knew better. On Atlantica, mysterious sapphire-hued illumination *meant* something. In this case, he was pretty sure he knew what.

He ran. Straight toward Daria, keeping himself out of the snipers' lines of fire, but no longer concerned with making his approach surreptitious. The time for that was past.

Hugh noticed him before Daria did since the angle at which he stood was more conducive to seeing motion from the corner of his eye. He started to spin, half-freezing as he almost tried to fire the bizarre weapon in his right hand. Instead, he hoisted the M1 carbine in his left, firing two poorly-aimed shots.

Ty saw what was happening before it happened. He ducked and rolled, finding halfway decent cover behind a thick root and a portion of the ruined helicopter's roof as the rounds kicked up dirt behind and beside him.

Hugh cried, "Someone's flanked us!"

Ty rose from behind the metal sheet, surprised to notice that he was grinning. It was probably because Daria had finally noticed him.

"You idiot!" she shouted at Hugh. "He's with me. Don't you recognize him?"

The surviving Ashcroft squinted and blinked, then winced away and crouched as another volley of fire came from the surrounding jungle.

He retorted, "Well, he's not with *me.* Come out and show yourself!"

Ty was already crawling around the long way to get closer to Daria while making it harder for Hugh to shoot him unless he exposed himself to the Ghost-Makers. The second Executioner was near enough that he could judge her overall condition, even if he'd need to examine her more carefully to make sure she was all right.

She appeared battered and disheveled. Her hair was tousled and frayed, a nasty purple bruise showed beneath one torn shirt sleeve, and there was a line of scabbing across her throat from the shallow cuts where Tilda had held her hostage with the sickle blade. For having been in a helicopter crash, she didn't look too bad.

Ty emerged from cover and approached them openly. Hugh had given up trying to kill him and was focused again on the hidden marksmen. Still, Ty held his rifle ready to fire at a split second's notice.

He said to Hugh and Daria, "We're all in this together for the moment." His words from minutes earlier echoed within his skull about how the rigors of being in combat made enemies into the best of friends with astounding speed.

Hugh laughed again in a way that threw his sanity into serious question. "Jolly good!" He used a fake, exaggeratedly posh British accent. The contrast was obvious next to his natural, default way of speaking, mostly Mid-Atlantic with a touch of Southern—about what Ty would've expected from an old-money society type from Maryland.

While Ty sidled up to Daria and tried to scan the woods for the locations of their mutual foes, Hugh produced a small case, held it to his face, and snorted something from it. Then he threw it aside and stared at Ty, exclaiming, "Executioner, watch this!"

Daria's expression turned alarmed. "Not again! You—"

Ty knew what was coming. He ducked, grabbed Daria's wrist, and pulled her down beside him.

Hugh sprang up from behind his cover of twisted metal and fired the weird makeshift handgun. The strange sonic report, not quite a "sound" but painful in its obscure intensity, filled the air, followed by a tremendous *crack*. Ty opened his mouth to equalize the pressure in his head as a blue light flashed from the gun's barrel.

A ripple of motion went across the glade and into the thickest part of the jungle, where at least one of the Ghost-Makers seemed to be hiding. Static crackled around Ty, and he blinked, his eyes filling with tears for no identifiable reason. Through the moisture screen, he saw trees shattering and toppling as the beam shredded the underbrush to a cloud of green snow. The line of devastation extended far into the forest.

Hugh cackled. "Play ball with the big boys, and you get the big-boy *toys*. Ha!" His pupils had grown to enormous size so they seemed to swallow the blue irises of his bulging eyes. Trickles of blood ran freely from his ears.

Small arcs of bluish lightning were snapping around the bizarre weapon, leaving pitted burns on Hugh's hand, but he didn't seem to notice. He'd screamed his taunt at the top of his lungs. Ty might not have heard or comprehended it otherwise, given how his ears rang. It was as though the blast had turned the air into liquid.

Ty yelled, "We need to leave." He could barely hear his voice. Daria was right next to him, her face growing red as she shouted at Hugh to get back under cover, yet she sounded half a klick away.

The rifle fire from behind the brush had stopped when Hugh Ashcroft fired his weapon. However, the blast hadn't taken them all out.

A .308 bullet, its report muffled in the wake of the devastating pulse, ripped through the air and found its mark near the juncture of Hugh's throat and chest. It blasted out his collarbone in a spray of blood.

CHAPTER FOURTEEN

His mad laughter transformed briefly into a sharp scream, then a wordless gurgle. Hugh tumbled to the side, dropping the carbine as his left hand clawed feebly at the air. His right hand remained clenched around the handle of his ray gun. He landed with a heavy *thud*. The bullet had missed his spine but had likely destroyed multiple veins and arteries and possibly his windpipe. If he wasn't dead by the time he hit the ground, he would be in another minute or so.

"Shit!" Ty cursed, gritting his teeth and ducking lower as further shots stitched across their position, blasting chunks and scraps from their ever-diminishing cover.

The Ghost-Makers were an especially aggressive species of sharpshooters. It seemed to be part of their modus operandi to deal with hard-to-get targets by simply harassing them with as much fire as they had ammo to spare and claim their kills when at last their victims made a mistake.

Even Ty found it nerve-wracking. The plus side was that it gave them a chance to escape, rather than blundering into a silent and peaceful scene and finding their heads blown off before they knew what had happened.

Of course, he had no intention of sticking around long enough for *any* of the snipers' tactics to work. Debriefing Daria and making sure she wasn't hurt worse than he'd estimated, taking grim satisfaction in Hugh's messy demise…all could come later. Once the crew of homicidal marksmen was far behind them.

He grabbed Daria's arm, the unbruised one. "We leave *now*."

She shot him an irritated glance. To his surprise and bewilderment, she tried to pull away from him and pointed first at Hugh's ravaged body, then at what remained of the chopper's cockpit.

"First, we need that weapon," she insisted. "There's a trunk inside the helicopter. We must have them."

He stared at her as though she'd suggested they dance a naked jig by the stream. "The hell we do."

Shaking her head and flapping her good hand, Daria tried to explain, in a raw and tired voice, "It's stuff from the Coven. Don't you see? We need to have it and study it to know what we're up against."

Her meaning and intent registered a flicker of appreciation within his mind, but mostly Ty was too keyed up, too deep into survival mode to have time for such concerns. "*Right now*, what we're up against is a fire team, maybe a whole squad, of angry professional killers. That's more important than the goddamn Coven."

Before the words had fully left his mouth, he knew it was useless. Daria had that stubborn look in her eye. She would fight against him every step of the way if he tried to drag her off without making an effort to get the case and the gun. If they survived, she would make the rest of his life a living hell anyway.

So he already found himself scanning the area around them, attempting to assess the best, safest, and sanest route to get to and recover the two items. There wasn't much time.

Their cover was sufficient for the moment. It consisted of

pieces of warped and scorched metal, thick layers of wood, and half-broken sheets of supposedly bulletproof glass. However, the Ghost-Makers continued to chip away at it. Neither the H-13's wreckage nor the natural obstacles of the jungle provided *enough* cover for them to stand straight without exposing themselves to enemy fire.

Ty glanced at the trunk. It was a black, bulky thing, heavy-looking and incongruous amid the debris, mostly hidden under a frayed, upside-down seat. It would be far more difficult to drag away from the crash site. Daria was smaller and less muscular than he was, and he feared it might slow her down.

He hesitated before making a dash for it. The experimental gun, or whatever it was, presented other problems.

It lay right near the edge of the main, makeshift wall of metal behind which they hid, still in Hugh's dead hand. Anyone who tried to snatch it up would put themselves in clear sight of a rifle scope. Speed might still save them, but the risk was enormous.

Ty also realized for the first time that Daria wore only her ripped shirt and trousers. The Ashcrofts had stripped off her armor at some point. Where it was and what they'd done with it, he had no idea.

His armor had taken several heavy bullets today. It was tough and wasn't specifically falling apart yet, but it wouldn't take much more punishment to compromise its integrity. It was strong enough to repel a projectile as fearsome as the .308 Winchester or .30-06 Springfield if it had to, but Atlantican body armor was primarily designed for protection from weaker stuff like handgun rounds or buckshot. At that, it excelled.

Under a barrage of full-power rifle cartridges, its effective-ness became a crapshoot.

He was still far better protected than Daria. Plus, he hadn't gone through all this to let her get killed by taking a stupid chance.

"Okay." He tried to lower his voice somewhat as his hearing

began to return to normal or as close as could be expected in a gunfight. He held Daria's arm firmly. She looked at him with impatience but then calmed a little when she saw that he was simply about to offer a plan. "I'm going to pop up and lay down some covering fire. You get that trunk, get out as fast as possible, and *stay down*. Then I'll get that gun-thing. Got it?"

As though she'd considered the same things he had, namely the trunk's weight, her face briefly scrunched up in an odd look of uncertainty, but then she nodded. "Yes, yes, fine."

Before he did anything else, Ty glanced back the way he'd come from. "Where is Amahle when I could use her?" he mumbled. There was no sign of the South African anywhere. She might've been watching, or she might've fled, or she might be doing something completely beyond his comprehension. That, too, was a question to address later.

Daria asked, "What? Who?"

"Never mind," Ty grunted. "You ready?" He flicked the selector switch on his rifle to full auto. The AR-10 handled almost more like a full-sized machine gun when firing automatically, making it difficult to control except in short bursts. In this case, accuracy wasn't the point.

Daria nodded and braced herself, ready to sprint toward the fallen seat and the remainder of the cockpit. It wasn't far away, but any distance was too much when enemy fire was incoming.

Ty did a final scan of the jungle to reassess the Ghost-Makers' most likely positions. Then he rose to his knees, brought his rifle up, and flexed his legs to spring past the upper edge of the steel sheet with as much speed as he could muster, aiming the AR-10's barrel at the area of jungle with the most direct line of fire toward his position.

"Eat this," he snarled, ignoring the bullet that whizzed past his shoulder close enough to fray one of the straps of his armor, and squeezed the trigger.

Daria scrambled across the mud behind him as the gun

barked and shook in his hands, spewing flame as Ty discharged nearly ten rounds in a tight but sweeping circle. Then he aimed to the sides and blasted off another five or six each, covering the woods with hot lead.

Due to the size of the rounds it fired, the AR-10's magazine held only twenty, less than the capacity of many submachine guns or the newer Soviet Kalashnikov rifles. The gun *clicked*, having emptied its mag quicker than Ty would've liked.

Then two shots rang off to his left. His hearing was still iffy due to the residual effects of Hugh's prototype weapon as well as the din of regular gunfire. Still, the sharp *crack* was distinct enough that he could tell it was firing *away* from him and toward the jungle, buying him an extra second to reload.

Amahle had joined the fray.

Grinning, ejecting his empty magazine, and slamming in a second, Ty again peppered the forest with 7.62 spearpoints. The snipers had stopped firing under the barrage. This time he gave them about half the magazine, saving the rest. He dropped back down behind cover and looked for Daria.

He and Amahle had bought her enough time. She'd scampered across the muddy expanse and ducked behind a half-dome of windshield glass, falling prone to wrestle the trunk free of its temporary resting spot. The weight was giving her trouble at such an awkward angle. However, she had hold of it, and she was out of the line of fire.

Off to the left, the South African began firing again when her former partners did. Rifle rounds streaked across the glade, their paths crisscrossing. One struck the metal right behind Ty's back and sent a shudder through him. As Amahle aimed careful shots into the jungle, enemy fire dissipated.

With her covering him, Ty sprang up again, fired a short burst of three rounds randomly into the forest, and dove straight for Hugh's body. He landed in the bloody dirt next to it, laid his rifle aside, and snatched the cobbled-together gun.

His hand wrapped around the "collar" of the weapon, above the grip and near the back of the receiver, so that once he jerked it free from the lifeless hand, he could hold it properly. The coils of copper wire and strange protrusions of metal toward the barrel gave him pause.

Unfortunately, Hugh still held the damn thing in a literal death grip. As Ty jerked on it more forcefully, a bullet sailed over his head and almost parted his hair. And Hugh pulled back.

"Oh, fuck," Ty breathed. Hugh Ashcroft wasn't dead.

The other man rolled onto his side, his body shuddering and his face lighting up with a livid mixture of pain, anger, and crazed confusion, while his white-knuckled right hand stopped pulling against Ty and instead pushed the gun back toward him.

"Ha," Hugh gasped, his voice wet and thin. "No one in my family knows how to die. Dying is for people like—"

Ty pounced on him, his left hand still trying to control the weapon, and whatever Hugh was about to say was lost in a fit of choking as the two men wrestled in the dirt. Hugh's legs kicked against the sheet of chopper metal while Ty attempted to reposition himself so he could pin Hugh's arm beneath him and draw his pistol.

The maddened former hunter had more strength left in his body than seemed right, given the horrible red gash running from the bottom of his Adam's apple to the top of his ribcage. With a sputtering heave, he regained control of the gun and squeezed the trigger—right as it was pointing *away* from Ty.

Ty rolled away, covering his ears and opening his mouth as the subsonic or supersonic pulse and the sharp, deafening *crack* came again. The gun's invisible blast all but vaporized the section of steel that protected them both from the Ghost-Makers. Beyond the smoking metal, it pulverized turf and roots before cutting another swath of destruction through the woods on the clearing's far side.

When Ty turned back, dreading the impact of a rifle round at any second, he saw Hugh tottering on one knee, grinning and drooling blood. The ray gun continued to spew random tiny bolts of electricity, and he finally dropped it into the mud.

Then, his smile faded, his face went slack, and he toppled over on his back, the hole in his throat shooting up a final jet of blood. The wound had claimed him. He might have the last laugh, though, given how much worse he'd made everything before his death.

The fallen experimental pistol continued to react, vibrating as the blue glow intensified and more sparks and bolts of azure lightning leapt out from between the cracks.

"Holy hell," Ty gasped. As though the situation wasn't bad enough, he finally realized exactly what was happening. As he'd suspected, Atlanticore crystals powered the ray gun. Usually dormant, they became highly unstable under certain circumstances—at which point they made dynamite look like a child's firecracker. He'd destroyed an entire boat with one around the time he first became an Executioner.

There might not be much time. He pivoted to the side and shouted with as much force as possible. He couldn't hear his voice except in the most muffled and indistinct way, since Hugh's last point-blank shot had brutalized his ears even with them covered.

"Daria! Get under cover and get the hell out of here. Amahle is with me. Go!"

He jumped to his feet only to crouch again, scrambling ape-like toward the fallen crystal-powered gun. One of the snipers took a shot that mostly missed, grazing the edge of his shoulder plate. On the plus side, Ty saw the muzzle flash from the corner of his eye. The sniper was well-hidden but closer than he'd guessed.

He reached down and grabbed the ray gun. Immediately his hands screamed with pain, the effect of the crackling blue energy like a cross between taking hold of heated metal and getting a static electricity shock from a doorknob. He nearly dropped it but forced his hands to retain their hold.

Only for a second. Long enough to throw it.

Everything seemed to be happening at once, yet he *felt* the eyes of at least one of the Ghost-Makers directly on him as he raised the shuddering weapon and looked at the trees.

With his sense of time distorted, Ty couldn't be sure if his arm moved first or if the sniper squeezed the trigger first, but it was close either way. He heaved the Atlantican ray gun into the woods toward the closest marksman. At approximately the same time, another of his opponents fired.

While the gun sailed in a broad arc across the glade toward the densest part of the tree line, another muzzle blazed, and a quick volley of two shots smashed directly into Ty's chest. He'd dropped his weak-side foot back when throwing the gun and was in a stable enough position that the bullets failed to knock him on his back.

Instead, they inflamed the pain of his earlier injury, threw him off-balance, hammered the air out of his lungs, and caused him to topple and twist partway to the side in tandem with dropping to his knees. He prayed that his armor hadn't yet completely given up the ghost.

There was no time to examine it. The prototype weapon, its internal power source of Atlanticore crystal no longer able to take the stresses placed upon it, exploded in midair.

The bright blue flash's nexus was right past the tree line, perhaps a yard in front of the sniper who'd dug in there. At first there was only a blue-white sphere, bright as the sun and about the size of a cottage. Then the whole glade seemed illuminated as if by a flash of lightning directly overhead, and the air cracked open with a furious clangor, even louder than the reports when Hugh had fired the gun.

Ty felt an invisible force push him back and up, picked up and tossed through the air. The explosion let out a massive shockwave of concussive force. There was also a bizarre sensation of it trying to pull him in simultaneously, as though oscillating fields of opposing gravity were striving against one another.

Trees turned to sawdust, and the sawdust spun and cycled around in miniature whirlwinds that moved to and fro without rhyme or reason. Clods of earth, still showing the burning roots that had grown through the bottom, were blasted up into the air to disintegrate. The atmosphere itself appeared to burn with blue fire.

The last thing he saw before he blacked out was Daria's face, contorted in horror, probably screaming. He heard nothing at all.

CHAPTER FIFTEEN

Tyler Katakura awoke in what had to be a different world. It was cold, dark, and suffocating. It bore no resemblance to the relatively warm and lush hills and forestlands of Atlantica, which, for all their mist-shrouded promise of menace, were beautiful and full of fresh, invigorating, breathable air.

He thought he might be in a cave or a deep basement. Alternatively, there was another possibility.

The bullets crashing into his chest atop his earlier wounds, combined with the tremendous blast of the exploding crystal weapon, had finished him off. His present environs felt like another world because they were—he'd arrived in the depths of the land of the dead.

"No," he gasped, as much for the sake of being able to hear his voice as anything else. "That makes no sense. I can talk. I'm...somewhere. I have to be alive. My fucking chest still hurts. Think of that, Tyler. Reach out. Find something and touch it."

He did. His arm, intact and functional, extended and came down with a handful of mud.

"Don't panic," he ordered himself. "There's no mud in hell, probably. Seems like it would be pointless." He couldn't completely banish the sense that something was terribly wrong, that he was injured and alone in hostile territory.

That even if he was still among the living, he might not be for much longer.

His ears were working again. That, too, was a good sign, although they still rang and smarted with the painful abuse of everything he'd subjected them to during the earlier gunfight. Absentmindedly, he wondered how bad his hearing would end up being if, by some miracle, he lived to old age.

He had other concerns, though. His whole body was afire with pain, both deep aches of the kinds that accompanied serious muscle damage and the searing sting of burns and lacerations. Plus, something was pressing down on him. Whatever it was, it weighed enough that it seemed to be gradually crushing his body.

"What did I ever do," he gasped, almost chortling, "to deserve this enough that I, uh, punished myself like this?"

On the positive side, the cool, wet mud offered partial solace to the burns on his hand, from where he'd carelessly grabbed the ray gun before it had exploded. It still throbbed. The pain was a low buzz, like the growl of a dog, threatening worse things to come.

In fact, mud was everywhere. He seemed to be lying right on the bank of a body of running water. Probably the stream he'd crossed earlier before reaching the wrecked chopper and trying to save Daria.

That raised the question, though—why was it so dark?

"Nighttime," he muttered. "I was out all afternoon. Yeah. Right?"

He lifted his head and turned his neck from side to side. He blinked his eyes a few times to confirm that they were open, but it made virtually no difference. When opened, he could see the faintest hint of details around him, but it was otherwise almost pitch black.

The muscles in his lower abdomen contracted in time with a

cold spike of fear. The blast might've damaged his eyesight, perhaps permanently. There were legends of blind swordsmen in his parents' native country. A blind Executioner in modern Atlantica wouldn't be much good to anyone.

Ty reached out, feeling for hard surfaces or heavy objects. Anything he could use to pull himself up and away from the water, which felt colder every second. He didn't feel up to trying to get to his knees, let alone his feet, quite yet.

He found a jutted-out spike of rock or well-hardened dirt, clasped his hands around it, and dragged himself forward. Again, there was pain everywhere, but he could move. And his eyes were beginning to adjust.

He was underground.

"What the hell?" he mumbled. "How?" It made no sense. Unless there had been a cave more or less right under his feet or a grotto beside the stream, perhaps, and the explosion had caved in the earth and buried him here. Not an encouraging prospect. It was the only explanation that was remotely rational.

Over the next ten minutes, he explored his surroundings, more by touch than by sight, and found that he was indeed in a small hollow in the earth, partially natural but mostly created by the blast.

The water from the stream seeped in near the edge in a slow gurgle, without any significant air gap between it and the surrounding ground. Ty stuck his arm into the flow and found that it was coming through a crack too narrow for him to be able to swim to freedom. He might use the stream as a weak point to dig himself out, but there didn't appear to be an easy way out of his situation.

Once his body's sensations returned, and he got over the ache that always accompanied the return to consciousness, he discovered that he wasn't in as bad a shape as he'd feared. He was beat to hell but not severely injured in any way that he could tell. For the time being, he was fortunate.

He wondered, what about Daria? What about Amahle? Certainly, neither of them were in the cave-in beside him, and he had no idea where they might be. He tried not to dwell on the possibility that one or both of them might've been crushed or smothered in the same miniature landslide that had put him in the grotto.

Breathing in and out, he tried to think and calm his mind. There was a paradoxical clash between giddy joy at simply being alive and awful acidic fear that he might be trapped and his friends already dead.

He *probably* had time to figure something out and take action.

He had to get out of here. He wouldn't be able to do any good for himself or anyone else if he remained trapped under a jumbled pile of mud and general detritus. His enemies would come for him, sooner or later. Even if the Atlanticore explosion had killed all the Ghost-Makers firing on them from the glade, the organization had far more members waiting in the wings.

Furthermore, the oxygen seemed thin enough that there was a slim chance of suffocation if he stayed here too long. Or if more stuff collapsed on top of him, or if the rut he was in settled deeper into the ground, potentially allowing the stream to flood in and transform it into a well.

Ty scrambled up the gentle, muddy slope. Despite the near-total darkness, there had to be a point of egress somewhere around him. If not an actual opening, at least a point where the miscellaneous crap that had piled atop him was thin enough to break through.

Once he reached a spot next to a massive curling root where the darkness seemed less oppressively thick, he stopped crawling and scrounging around. He remained silent, listening to everything around him for the slightest hint of anything that might be useful.

He heard the gentle rush and gurgle of the water. Outside was the faint passage of a light breeze and what sounded like insects scratching and scrabbling in the dirt and over the wood and blasted metal.

There was something else, too. A human voice, calling out, not yet articulate enough to distinguish actual words or meaning.

Ty tensed. His brain buzzed with the need to decide while aching with the fact that he didn't yet have enough quality information to make a *good* decision. Any one of several paths might lead to death.

There was no way to be sure who the person or persons outside were. It might be his friends, or it might be the Ghost-Makers, or it could be some random farmer or traveler trying to figure out what had happened to wreak so much havoc across this stretch of the wilderness. If it was anyone hostile, he was in a badly compromised position and would be at a massive disadvantage if he tried to fight back or escape.

He mulled it over for a few seconds as the calls grew louder but no more articulate.

"No," he declared in a soft but firm voice. "I'm not sitting around in this tomb." Friend or foe, he would rather have the chance to face them in the sunlight than cower and suffer a slow death by suffocation or starvation down here in the murky dark.

He drew in a deep breath and bellowed, *"Hey!"* His voice sounded absurdly loud in the stuffy, confined space.

It seemed that outside, there was a pause in the shouts. Then they resumed, growing slightly closer.

Ty moved his hands around the walls and ceiling of his prison. Mostly he found earth, wood, and random stuff he couldn't identify. What he needed was steel.

It took about a minute, but he discovered some. A couple of girders from the chopper had twisted together like a pretzel and stuck down through the mass of half-dried mud. They'd lain in a patch of deep shadows and thus been invisible to him until now. He found them by touch.

"That's more like it," he muttered, finding and picking up a rock. He reared back and slammed it into the girders, beating on them again and again so a clear metallic ringing and clanging echoed through the makeshift cave.

Hopefully, it was making sound aboveground or at least sending vibrations through the earth that the people outside could feel or sense.

Ty didn't want to waste too much oxygen, but when it sounded like the calling voices grew louder, he shouted again, twice, hoping that they could hear him and trace the location of the sound to the same place where the metallic clangor was coming from.

A moment later, he noted heavy, rhythmic *thuds* moving closer to his position. Someone was jogging toward him. Then a male voice, muffled but finally comprehensible, asked, "Hey! Is someone down there?"

"Yeah," Ty yelled back. "Get me out of here, and we'll talk about it. I'll dig from my end."

He was about to ask who it was and perhaps identify himself but decided against it. There was the possibility that the men outside were Ghost-Makers who thought that he was one of their comrades. If that were the case, the shock of finding out who he was might give Ty a moment's advantage to take them out or get past them. If they were friendly, then no harm done, anyway.

Ty made sure his rifle's safety was on. Then he used the butt of the gun to begin digging out mud and dirt near the steel girders, approximately on the opposite side of the newly-formed cave wall from where the men outside had begun chopping and heaving away the debris.

It took about five minutes before the digging sounds grew loud enough and the dirt and rubble thinned to the point where Ty saw beams of white sunlight stream through. He'd done his part. A massive pile of earth lay behind him, having been tossed and strewn aside or back into the creek.

He stopped. He would wait for his rescuers to do the last of the work. That way, if anyone needed to get shot, Ty would be the one best-placed to do the shooting. He settled back on his knee and held his rifle's now-filthy stock to his shoulder, the muzzle pointed a bit down and to the side, but ready to raise and fire at a split second's notice should he need to.

Seconds later, the last of the piled-up dirt collapsed. Light flooded the little pseudo-cave, and Ty winced, grasping that the sun's sudden intrusion would all but neutralize the advantage he'd given himself due to how badly adjusted his eyes were.

A voice with a familiar New York accent said, "Holy shit, it's Ty!"

Another man with a South Asian accent added, "Ah, yes, we are lucky. We had feared it might be one of them."

Ty closed his eyes, exhaled, and allowed his gun to drop to the ground. He wanted to collapse from sheer relief. "Gage. Dante. Thank God... I was thinking the same thing. Pull me out of this damn hole so we can all figure out what the hell is going on."

"Agreed." Dante extended his long arms into the opening and seized Ty around the wrists, tugging back and up. Ty braced his feet and scrambled up the slope. It wasn't easy since the ground was so soft and full of so many random obstacles, but he trod enough mud to get his upper half back into the fresh air. At that point, Gage joined in, wrapping his arms around Ty's waist and hauling him up onto a patch of burned grass.

It was daytime, but the sun was waning. Ty guessed that he'd only been unconscious for a short time, perhaps around an hour, but there was the chance he'd been out for a full day or more. He asked his friends about it.

"No," Gage reassured him. "You and the woman went up the hill late this morning. It is still the same day. We haven't found her yet. We have Daria, however. She's not in the best condition, but she's alive and will recover."

Ty exhaled. "Okay. Good." A pang of concern for Amahle interrupted his relief but knowing Daria had made it was his first concern. "Tell me everything that happened. Start from the beginning. Meaning, from when you left Amahle and me behind."

Dante ran his hands over Ty's shoulders and back. "Sure, but let me check you first. Doesn't look like you got too badly hurt, but some trauma or damage. Were you caught in an explosion? That's what it looks like based on the surroundings."

Ty glanced around. The earth was torn up, scorched, and cratered, and trees had fallen or shattered. The glade looked like someone had subjected it to an aerial bombing campaign. The stream still flowed, but it looked as though all the damage to the ground had permanently altered its course and its current strength.

"Yeah," he grunted. "Atlanticore. I'll tell you all about it soon. First, fill me in on what happened on your end."

While Dante examined and prodded him, pausing to produce disinfectant and gauze to wrap around the worst of his abrasions, Gage explained the events of the last half a day.

He and Dante had gone straight back to the Executioners' headquarters in Atlantica Metro. Not long after they'd returned, they'd begun receiving reports and rumors—people who lived on the fringes of the city had been complaining about bizarre shock-waves in the air and loud, disturbing *cracking* sounds. Ty didn't interrupt, but he was sure his friends would be interested to know the true source of the disturbances.

After the third such report, Eleanor had called them and proclaimed that the Executives wanted them to check it out. They figured it was related to the unpleasantness involving the Ashcrofts and their sponsors, so they'd returned to a point as close as possible to the seeming origin of the sound...after confirming that it wasn't far from where they'd dropped Ty and Amahle off a few hours previously.

Gage sighed. "We tried to speak to Hugh and Tilda on the radio in the hope that they were still using the stolen Autocu-tioner. They didn't answer. Not during our drive into the hills, and not afterward, although we gave them a short time after we arrived in the jungle. So we parked our vehicle on a flat place not far from here and began to investigate on foot."

Ty winced as Dante continued to apply basic field medicine to his myriad wounds. "That sounds about right. I'm glad you were able to find me so fast. Did you see the explosion? Or hear it?"

Dante snorted. "Oh, yeah. It was pretty hard not to, bud."

Gage added, "We saw a tremendous flash of light followed by a most deafening *crack*, like what the people who live nearby had described. We headed straight toward it, and we found Daria and you. It's a relief that you are alive since we'd feared that nothing could survive such devastation. How did it happen? You mentioned Atlanticore."

Ty didn't think there was time to go into too much detail, but he told them briefly about the crash, the firefight, and the strange Atlanticore weapon. "It was practically burning itself to pieces when I picked it up," he concluded. "When it blew, I thought it was all over."

Dante had been kneeling beside him. Now he stood. "Well, that would explain the burns on your hand. Otherwise, you're not in too bad a shape. I patched up a couple of gashes that looked like they might be infection-prone, but I'll need the rest of my kit to deal with the rest. The good news is that it's not too far, and it's mostly downhill."

He and Gage helped Ty to his feet and watched him as they did a final walk-around of the blast site, looking for anything else they might've missed. Ty couldn't find the case that Daria had insisted was so important. Nor was there any sign of the snipers.

Gage commented, "We found Daria near the southern edge of this clearing. She was battered but otherwise all right. She is recovering as we speak."

Ty nodded. Things were bad, but not disastrous. He had a feeling that once he was able to speak to Ms. Barruk, he would be clearer on the nature of what lay ahead.

It took about half an hour or less to reach the vehicle. The clearing lay on a small natural terrace halfway down one of the gentler hills nearby, roughly midway between the crash site and the highway. Dante explained that they would've happily driven farther into the jungle to have spared everyone the extra hike, but the terrain was simply too rough.

Ty muttered, "Yeah, I know. The important thing is, you came. You rescued me right when I needed you."

Gage smiled. "Yes, we try our best. Unfortunately, we had to leave Daria alone, but she insisted that she would be fine and we should look for you."

That sounded exactly like her, Ty thought.

They'd parked the Autocutioner at the end of a pair of rutted tracks in a spot where the surrounding trees and brush gave it a certain amount of visual cover. Once they got close enough to it, its presence was obvious, but at least it would be hard to see from farther away. Or from the sky.

With darkness falling, they had the advantage of night on their side as well. So did their hidden enemies.

As they approached, Ty noted that Daria didn't jump out to greet them, which made him worry about her condition. Maybe she had a torn thigh muscle or a broken ankle or something. Or she might simply be sleeping while she had the chance, although he didn't like the thought of her being unconscious by herself while the Ghost-Makers were still out there, hunting for all their heads.

He turned to Dante. "I'd like to see Daria before we do anything else."

"I figured." He chuckled. "She's probably resting in the back."

They opened the vehicle's rear and found Daria sitting up from a makeshift bed, blinking and staring at them. Her eyes widened and fixed on Ty, then she relaxed, returning to her customary self-contained demeanor despite the undeniable warmth on her face.

Ty clambered up over the bumper and knelt beside her, ignoring the aches and pains of his various minor injuries. "Good to see you again under calmer circumstances. You've looked better, but probably also worse."

She had various cuts, scrapes, and light burns over her face, arms, and shoulders, and she was pale and haggard as though it were she who they'd pulled out of a moldy cave. Yet she'd also escaped anything that looked too much like a major, debilitating wound.

"Yes, yes." She waved. "You are much the same, I see. Here." She reached out, and suddenly they were embracing, maybe too tight for either of them. Neither spoke for half a minute. It was unnecessary to state aloud the obvious—that both were overjoyed simply to see the other alive.

As they drew apart, Ty's burned hand scraped over the sleeve of her jacket, and he winced, the air hissing between his teeth.

Daria's eyes snapped down. "Those are rather bad burns. Dante! Why haven't you bandaged his hand yet?"

Dante had gone around to the front cab while the pair hugged and brought out a medical kit. "Because I used up all the bandages I had on other stuff. Had to get back to my extra stash. Yeah, with second-degree burns there's a risk of infection, but he also had some open bleeding wounds that I had to deal with."

He examined Ty's hand. Ty looked at it too and noted how much worse it looked, somehow, under the electric light within the truck. It was mottled with red and white streaks, blisters, and blackened fringes. Yet the blazing pain as Dante wrapped it gave him consolation, in a way. The worst burns were the ones you couldn't feel—where the heat had gotten so deep into the flesh that it caused major nerve damage.

Ty shifted his mind away from his petty agonies. There were more important things to worry about.

"Daria," he began, "did you see Amahle? A South African woman about your size with scars on her face, carrying a rifle.

She was one of the shooters on our side back in the valley when the Ghost-Makers opened fire on us. For that matter, did you see or hear anything else?"

Dante snapped, "Hey! Hold still. I can't take care of your hand if you keep jerking it around like that."

Ty frowned and glanced aside at his friend. "Sorry. I get animated when I ask questions."

Daria paid no heed to the brief exchange. "I'm afraid I didn't see much. The explosion knocked me over, and I went in and out of consciousness several times. My ears were ringing, and I was dizzy, and I could barely move at first. I glimpsed people moving through the clearing. I didn't get a good look at them."

Ty's nod was slow and resigned. That was about what he'd expected to hear from her, but perhaps it was better than nothing. "Could you tell how many of them there were? What they were doing?"

She frowned and went on, "I'm not sure. They must have been the Ghost-Makers. I saw the silhouettes of at least two people, but there might have been more than that. They were dragging things away. I believe it was the bodies of other people. Whether they were dead or only knocked out, I don't know.

"It could've been that this Amahle woman was among them, or maybe it was some of their people whom we killed. I'm sorry. I cannot be of much help here."

Ty's jaw clenched. He didn't blame Daria, of course, but the angry, grating frustration was coming back. The last two or three days had been among the most trying of his life. Recently, at least.

Daria blinked and snapped her fingers. "Oh, one other rather important thing. The case is gone. The one with the Coven stuff, which we tried to recover. I couldn't find it after I woke up. They might well have taken it."

He sprang forward, not realizing until he was two steps past Daria that Dante hadn't finished bandaging his hand yet. Strips of gauze dangled from his wrist.

"Hey!" the physician exclaimed. "Goddammit, Ty, how do you expect me to do my job when you keep pulling this shit?"

Gage climbed into the back. "Now, now. You've done your part. It's not your fault that Ty sometimes forgets he is a human being who feels pain."

Tyler ducked through the doorway at the front of the rear compartment and swung into the passenger's seat. With his good hand, he flicked the "on" switch on the radio and unhooked the microphone, waiting for a response.

There was a vague increase in fuzzy static, but the delay took longer than usual. It was past dark, and he feared that no one might be in the office at this hour. "Come on," he grumbled.

Dante, having started after him, squeezed his upper half between the seats. "What are you doing, pal?"

Ty glanced at him and returned to staring at the radio. "We need to make a deal."

Behind Dante, Daria's voice asked, "With whom; if I might ask?" The words were arch and filled with that faint scoffing disdain she occasionally used when Ty suggested something crazy.

Ty ignored her for now. As much as he valued her intelligence and her suggestions, sometimes it was better to simply get his ideas rolling first and ask for everyone else's opinion second.

The voice of Eleanor Cervantes came through a moment later. She sounded tired and exasperated, as though she'd been working all day and was about to go home and rest—or as though she dreaded the prospect of having to hear whatever the Executioners were about to tell her.

"Hello, this is Eleanor. How can I help you? Over."

"This is Katakura," Ty began, using his firmest and most businesslike tone. "We've had some serious problems, but we're all alive. Listen, Eleanor, I know it's late, but this is important. We need you, or someone you trust, to find a way to contact the Ghost-Makers. Can you do that? Over."

The brief stretch of awkward silence suggested that Eleanor wasn't pleased by the notion. "I should be able to, yes. What is the message? Over."

Ty inhaled and relaxed his mind. "Tell She-Wolf that we're willing to make her an offer. We can give her a deal for Amahle Nikoze, at least as good as what she and her crew got for Hugh and Tilda Ashcroft."

His instincts told him that they'd captured Amahle. There was no specific evidence, no way to confirm it. It was the explanation that made the most sense, though. They hadn't found Amahle's body, nor had the woman made any effort to find them or contact them.

Since it had been a couple of hours, at least, She-Wolf might've already put her rebellious protege to death. Or she didn't have Amahle at all and might simply bluff the Executioners in the hope of ripping them off.

Eleanor made a low humming sound. "Mm, yes, I can try that, but I'm not certain it will work. The message might have to go through several layers of intermediaries, which will slow it down. Is this Amahle person in danger? Over."

"Yes. Over."

Reluctantly, Eleanor agreed to do all she could to expedite Ty's offer and to get back with the team once she had more information for them. Then she inquired about how the mission had gone and if there was anything else she needed to know.

Ty told her, "Hugh and Tilda are dead. We couldn't raid the lodge for any evidence because we had other priorities. Daria and I have taken some wounds, but nothing that will keep us out of action—I think—or require hospitalization so far. In addition to trying to kill us, the Ghost-Makers might be our best lead as far as tying up all the loose ends in this case. It's imperative that we find out where they are and talk to them. Over."

"I see," Eleanor confirmed. "I will do everything I can. Please keep someone near your radio at all times. Good luck. Out."

As her voice faded, Ty turned backward. Dante was right there, and Daria and Gage had crowded up behind him near the threshold of the door dividing the cab from the rear compartment.

Dante cleared his throat. "Okay, what's going on? Making the people who tried to kill us a 'better offer' for a sniper lady we just met? I'm not saying you're wrong, only that you have some info we don't."

Ty's impatience was rising again, but Dante had a point. He needed the whole team working together, and that meant bringing them into the loop and explaining both his motivations and his strategies.

"All right," he began, "here's what's up. Amahle Nikoze saved my life. Her former comrades want to kill her, so if she's still alive, I refuse to abandon her, and none of you are going to convince me otherwise. There's more to it than that, but I want to get that out of the way first."

No one objected, despite a flicker of uncertainty on their faces, so he went on.

"Second, the Ghost-Makers might be our ticket to finding out more about the Coven of Miracles. If we can capture some of them, they might divulge information we can use. Not to mention, they failed to complete the contract hit on us while using Coven technology. They got whatever was in that trunk. So the Ghost-Makers might have *other* people coming after *them.* The Coven seems to have a scorched earth policy regarding anyone who angers them. It's a volatile situation but one that might finally point us in the right direction."

He paused and breathed. "I might not be able to do it alone. With all four of us, though...the odds are a lot better."

The blank way they stared back at him in reflective concern made him feel oddly frightened and alone. He was so used to ignoring the feeling that he'd managed to pretend it didn't exist for lengthy periods of his life. But abandonment and failure were always something to fear.

Daria was first to break the silence. "I owe this Amahle my life, then, as do you." She brushed a lock of hair away from her wan face. "She helped you locate me. I wouldn't have made it by myself, between Hugh being a madman and the Ghost-Makers moving in for the kill. I will accompany you, Mr. Katakura."

Gage raised a finger. "I do believe we had a deal with Ms. Nikoze. That if we found Daria and brought her back alive, then she was to be made an Executioner."

Dante nodded. "Yeah. I mean, if she's already dead, at least we tried. Still, we should keep our word. She came through, didn't she?"

No one spoke. In a rough circle, they all looked into one another's eyes, the gravity of their commitment to each other sinking in. With it came a faint excitement—the prospect of unraveling the mystery of the Coven.

The radio crackled. Ty swiveled around, flinched in pain as the motion strained one of the cuts on his torso, and grabbed the microphone. "Hi, it's Tyler. Over."

"Katakura," Eleanor greeted him. "It didn't take nearly as long as I thought. I believe the Ghost-Makers *expected* to hear from us. I have the details of how they wish to set up a meeting. Over."

Ty glanced at his friends. To them, he spoke in a low voice while covering the mic. "Time to get one of our own back." Then he addressed Eleanor. "Okay. Go ahead."

CHAPTER SIXTEEN

The meeting time was twenty-three hours past the point at which Eleanor called them back. Ty wasn't sure how he felt about it. He could use some time to rest and recover after everything he'd been through. On the other hand, giving She-Wolf and her people almost a full day to prepare meant that the Ghost-Makers would be able to stack the odds even more greatly in their favor.

If they'd indeed already killed Amahle, it would be easier for them to cover it up and concoct a way to fool the Executioners in the meantime.

Begrudgingly and roiling with worries and uncertainties, the four of them had returned home to their HQ to recuperate and prepare for the worst.

Much of what they needed to do couldn't be done until the morning when they heard the rest of the details from Eleanor and received the ransom payment. So, they spent that evening doing the stuff they *could* accomplish that would still be useful.

First, Dante looked over everyone's wounds in more detail and tended to them with his full stock of medical gear. He'd established a respectable infirmary within the station that was almost on par with a proper hospital ward, minus some of the most specialized equipment.

Next, they checked to ensure their vehicles were in working order. Ty and Daria noted with approval that either Gage or Dante had located the other Autocutioner and brought it back to base. Both trucks were somewhat roughed up from the drive through the wooded hills but otherwise in good functional shape.

Finally, they cleaned and oiled their weapons and gathered their ammo reserves while comparing notes on all they'd learned.

Ty ignored the pain in his right hand and used it to hold his AR-10 magazines while loading 7.62 rounds into them with his left. He also checked to ensure his 1911 pistol was loaded, with a couple of spare mags' worth of .45 ACP on the side for good measure. His wakizashi's edge needed a touch-up thanks to his using it like a machete in the jungle, but it would suffice for now. He also slipped a small folding knife into his belt.

Addressing the others, he began, "Amahle told me that there might be at least two, maybe more like three dozen Ghost-Makers. She's not certain since they mostly work in semi-independent cells of three shooters. I don't know if all of them are on Atlantica, but we have to assume that She-Wolf, their leader, is going to have as many marksmen with her as she can."

Daria agreed. "That seems a fair assumption. It will be difficult to find out their numbers before we walk into a trap. For snipers, they're unusually fond of laying down a heavy volume of fire. Their stealth abilities are formidable. None of us noticed them hiding in the woods around the valley when we went to deliver Hugh and Tilda to the farmers." She cleaned gunpowder residue from the barrel of her Uzi.

Dante grumbled, "Yeah, well, this time we know they'll be there. I'm guessing the meeting won't be in the jungle. They might not have as many places to hide. Hell, maybe we'll get lucky, and they'll cluster together to try to intimidate us with their numbers like a street gang or something." He tested the pump on his Ithaca shotgun and loaded it with shells of 12-gauge buckshot.

Rubbing his chin and pressing .455 Webley rounds into a speed loader for his revolver, Gage mused, "That seems most unlikely. Perhaps they will have a group confront us, but they will have someone on overwatch. At least two, I would imagine." He snapped the gun shut and put both of his kukris in their sheaths.

Daria waved vaguely. "There is little more we can do tonight. We should all get some rest so we're in good condition. Come the morning, we'll know more and can make the rest of our preparations then."

Ty had to admit she was right. Still, even after locking the place up tight and double-checking all of their alarms and security systems, sleep didn't come easily.

The next day, as the four of them ate breakfast and drank their tea or coffee, Eleanor Cervantes stopped by along with one of her assistants and one of the security officers from MacLeod's team.

"Good day," Eleanor greeted them as Ty answered the door, pistol held low in his hand. "We've brought the money along with a transcript of their instructions. And a map and blueprints of the area where you'll be making the trade."

Her assistant held up a secure suitcase, doubtless loaded with cash. If the Executives were remotely as smart as Ty hoped they were, it also held a tracking device of some sort.

He nodded. Now was when the real games would begin.

CHAPTER SEVENTEEN

The meeting place was an industrial dockyard along Atlantica's east coast. It was about twelve miles from the city's edge and adjacent to a newer rural settlement. However, the docks were already doing enough business that the little village might burgeon into a town, or even a second city, within the next several years.

For the sake of the community's safety and everyone else involved, the Executives had arranged to clear the place of people, boats, and activities of all types. They were to wrap up business and have everyone gone by dark. The Executives also rerouted ships scheduled to arrive that evening to the main city docks farther southwest along the coast.

Tyler had tried to press Eleanor for intel on how many people She-Wolf would have with her and what their setup would be, but unsurprisingly the Ghost-Makers had refused to divulge that, and none of the Execs' people knew it offhand, either. The only thing the sniper company had said was that they wanted Ty to do the transfer, that he would be meeting directly with their leader, and that "someone" would be watching at all times.

This meant that they would probably have every shooter they

could spare holed up somewhere nearby with scopes trained on the docks. Not to mention at least one or two scouts ensuring that the Executioners didn't sniff around the area too closely and remove the snipers beforehand.

As the truck rumbled along the coast road, leaving behind the fringes of Atlantica Metro and entering the countryside that lay beyond, Ty looked down again at the briefcase and patted it.

Five hundred thousand U.S. dollars in cash. Half a million. Ty wondered how the sum compared to whatever the Coven had offered the Ghost-Makers for their secondary contract against the people-hunters. It was probably of a similar amount, and She-Wolf had reasoned that doubling her profits would be worth the loss of a single treasonous former member.

According to Eleanor, though, the Executives hadn't been particularly happy about it. In the end, they'd put up the funds. As their spokeswoman had put it, "Our benefactors have expressed their fervent hope that having to pay ransoms will not become a repeated or common occurrence. We don't wish it known that we'll negotiate with terrorists and simply pay money to anyone who threatens us."

Ty completely understood the sentiment. Paying out created an incentive for other people to try the same shit, figuring it would be easy money. Under these circumstances it was the best option they had.

"If all goes well," he'd told Eleanor, "we—meaning my team, you, and the Executives all—will be getting more than our money's worth."

As they drew closer to the docks, Ty blinked and tried to focus his thoughts. He still hurt, and he was still tired. He'd only slept for about five or six hours. Given how badly beat up he was, nine would've been far better. It was enough for him to function. Part of him, buried deeply where no one else could see it, cringed in fear at the thought of the trouble he might have if anything went awry.

Still, his mind was sharp. They'd reviewed blueprints, diagrams, and photographs of the shipyard and its surrounding environs, to better plan how they would approach the whole endeavor. He'd drunk a single cup of strong tea. Enough to spike his alertness, but not enough to strain his bladder or make him jumpy.

The sun's last rays were fading beyond the western horizon, and deep blue darkness fell over the sky. Gage turned to his companions. "We will be there soon."

"Right." Ty looked at each of the three in turn. "Let's review the plan. We drop Daria off outside town so she can be our ace in the hole if things go bad."

He didn't like the thought of using her in such a strenuous and dangerous role, but since she was the one with the best alibi of being wounded, it would be easier to get away with claiming that they'd left her behind in a safe location in the city. If the Ghost-Makers saw only three of them instead of four, they might otherwise know something was up.

Daria quipped, "It might be that I'm more like a jack in the hole if I understand the metaphor correctly. Yes, I've been to this dockyard before. I believe they've expanded it since then. But I'm familiar with it, so I know the best places to hide."

Ty nodded. He kept to himself his one great concern, which was that Daria wasn't an overly accomplished markswoman with a rifle. It made sense to have a sniper to oppose other snipers. Still, she could shoot well enough at closer range and with pistol-caliber weapons. He had to trust her competence at making a long shot or two. If that failed, she could always use her subma-chine gun and a couple of smoke grenades to create a diversion.

Dante chimed in, "We'll wait in the truck. I don't like it, but it'll do. Gage and I took over that compound with him driving and me riding shotgun—literally, haha—so if we have to do something similar here, we will."

Gage raised a finger. "However, that was entirely on dry land.

Here we will be in narrower confines with the sea before us. I'm afraid I'll have to be more careful in how I drive if it comes to that. We might need to park the truck and engage with hand-to-hand weapons."

Dante shrugged. "Fine." He sounded disappointed. Still, he checked his shotgun to ensure it was loaded and in safe working order. Then for good measure he rolled his window down and back up and practiced getting into a firing position quickly, should the situation call for it.

Ty didn't talk much. The bulk of the responsibility would lay with him. He didn't think of himself as much of a negotiator. Still, successful execution of the mission would depend as much or more on his ability to speak, stall, and persuade as it would on any talent for violence.

His priority was ensuring that Amahle was alive. Second, buying them time and trying to get She-Wolf to reveal something, anything, about the Coven of Miracles that the Executioners could use later. If that didn't work, handing over the money and getting Amahle and himself out in one piece would have to suffice.

Beneath the stacks of bills, well hidden amid them, was a radio tracker. Ty or the Executives' other people would be able to tail the Ghost-Makers to wherever their hideaway on Atlantica was and get a lead on the Coven that way if need be.

The Autocutioner's headlights illuminated a low gate up ahead. Gage slowed down.

"Stop," Ty instructed him. "We have a good alibi. We're checking those gates before we drive into them. Daria, do your thing. Good luck."

The Polish woman nodded and slipped out the back. She made virtually no sound, and the shadows of dusk blanketed the bumpy terrain, providing plenty of cover. Then the truck moved forward and through the gates into the ramshackle little town.

A few people milled about, but for the most part, things were quiet—with the docks rendered inactive, there wasn't much for the locals to do. The bulk of them seemingly had retired to their homes to eat or speakeasies to drink.

The buildings receded, aside from a couple of warehouses, as the docks proper came into view. Beyond them, the starlight glinted off the choppy waters of the Atlantic.

Ty raised his hand, signaling Gage to stop the truck again.

"Okay, this is where I get out. Park here, or close to here. Don't do anything except sit, wait, and watch. Keep an eye out for anyone on the roof of that warehouse or hiding anywhere else, although you guys have the advantage of a heavily armored vehicle. They seem to use .308 rifles mostly, and even if they have a 50-cal, you'll probably be safe. If they try anything... Do whatever you have to. Daria will be sneaking up on that point over there, and we'll all need a lift. All five of us."

He gestured toward a low wall next to a couple of shrubs that lay on a small hillock, the obvious place for Ms. Barruk to perform her counter-sniper activities. Ty only hoped she could sneak through the town in time to help them should things go south.

The three men wished each other luck. Then Ty climbed out, carrying the briefcase in one hand. The Ghost-Makers had insisted that he leave his rifle behind. It languished in the Autocutioner, but he still had his 1911, wakizashi, and folding knife.

The sea breeze was oddly pleasant, and the night cool but not yet chilly. No one else was around. Ty walked straight out toward the main dock area, then veered right toward the second pier down. That was the agreed-upon place. He tried to look into every nook and cranny he passed without being too obvious about it.

He stood before Pier Five and waited. Thus far, there was no sign that the Ghost-Makers had shown up. After five minutes, his skin crawled with the prospect that it was all a setup—that She-Wolf planned to put a bullet in his head, blow up the Autocutioner with dynamite, and take the money without bothering to return Amahle. Who might already be dead, anyway.

A dark shape moved out on the horizon. A ship. It couldn't be coming this way…it was probably one of the cargo boats that was being rerouted to Atlantica Metro.

Then, from behind a broad wooden post that Ty could've sworn he'd already checked, out stepped a woman. Two women, the first dragging the second.

A brief flash of tension tightened his muscles, but he dispelled it almost at once with a deep breath and quick mantra. He couldn't see the women's faces yet or make out any details about their appearances, but it seemed fair to assume that showtime had begun.

The first woman had appeared with such a casual demeanor that it could only have been intentional. She wanted to get the drop on Ty without startling him. She'd succeeded.

Her right hand held a small gun, probably an old .32 break-top revolver. Not a particularly powerful weapon, but deadly enough in the hand of someone who knew how to shoot. Her left hand gripped the arm of the person in tow, who was halfway hunched over and carrying a large object of some sort.

Ty made no move. He stood and waited, watching.

The woman stepped forward so that, at last, her face came into the pale sodium light of the overhead lamp post. At the same time, so did the other person beside her.

Despite himself, Ty almost flinched. The individual standing before him could be no one other than She-Wolf, and she was aptly named.

He'd never seen such a fearsome-looking woman. He'd known women who were tough, capable, and ruthless when they had to be. Daria and Amahle were among them. Until he glimpsed the Ghost-Makers' leader, he didn't know that a human female *could* give off such an obvious first impression of being a stone-cold killer.

She was tall, about the same height as Ty, thin and rangy though suggesting lean whipcord muscle rather than simple svelteness. Her face was growing wizened but had a sharpness and hardness to it, with a default expression of fierce disdain. She had wiry gray hair that flowed from her head in a disheveled mop. The light glinted off a few strands that retained their color, a bright coppery red. Her remaining eye was bright green.

"So, then," she began in a gravelly parody of a musical Irish accent. "You've decided to show up. With the money too, I'm sure. You wouldn't be stupid enough to try to cheat me, now would you?"

Adding to her intimidating appearance was the damage done to her face by Amahle's sabotaged bullet. Fresh burns and scabbed-over cuts covered one cheek. Most tellingly, a makeshift patch covered her right eye. Ty wondered how well she could shoot with only the left.

Meanwhile, Amahle struggled in the grip of She-Wolf's left hand. They'd tied her wrists together, and her hands clamped around the handle of the trunk that Daria had tried to recover.

She wasn't well. The Ghost-Makers had beaten her severely, from the look of it. Bruises and dried blood covered her face and the way she shook suggested muscle cramps and perhaps fractured bones. For someone he'd known for such a short time, the sight of her in such a state sent cold waves of rage through Ty's brain.

He stared at She-Wolf. "I have the money. Five hundred thousand, as you requested. Now, I want to know—"

Before he could finish his inquiry, a horn sounded far out on the water. His eyes snapped toward it. Near the horizon, out across the water, was the silhouette of the ship he'd seen a moment ago, coming straight toward them and moving faster.

Ty turned his gaze back to She-Wolf, his anger rising and showing on his face. "The docks were to be cleared. We agreed to that."

The rangy woman snapped, "They *are* clear of people who have naught to do with this. Don't you worry, boyo, that's our ride off Atlantica. You don't expect us to stick around here once you've paid us, do you?"

In point of fact, that was precisely what the Executioners had hoped. That the Ghost-Makers would linger long enough to track them or intercept them before they could make their escape. They hadn't been able to plan for the prospect that She-Wolf would cheat on the details of their arrangement.

He had to buy them time. If Daria could sneak close enough, she could launch a surprise attack to derail the snipers' escape plans.

He pointed at the ship. "It wasn't in the deal. Neither was Amahle being beaten half to death. What the hell did you do to her? We're here to buy her safety."

Amahle looked at Tyler with a steady, inscrutable gaze. She wasn't trying to talk yet, and Ty couldn't tell what she might be thinking. Possibly, the abuse she'd suffered made it all but impossible for her to plan anything herself.

She-Wolf scoffed, "Hah! You're lucky not to be purchasing her mortal remains. Be thankful for what you can get of her, instead. We were about ready to finish her off when the call came in that someone thought she was worth a ransom payment."

The gray-haired woman looked at her protege with obvious snide disgust. "She must have got to you with her stupid idealistic ramblings—little-girl storybook stuff. I would've expected better from someone who came out of all the killing in South Africa.

"Well, we're the ones who will end up with the money. For all her attempted good deeds, she'll end up empty-handed and with only the fine company of you...people. Hah!"

"Yeah," Ty muttered, casually pretending to scan the waters, but he was checking for any signs of activity behind him through his peripheral vision. "Whatever. We'll take that deal. Except that by rights, we should dock your pay for how you've treated her."

She-Wolf responded by smacking Amahle on the head. The blow didn't have much force behind it, but it struck a sore spot on the younger woman's cheek, making her flinch.

Ty couldn't help himself. The sheer callous pettiness of it... He stepped forward.

She-Wolf snapped, "Watch it!" and raised her pistol. "Don't think I can't shoot straight because of the loss of one eye, my good man. I've used either when I had to. I'm deadlier with one than most ever will be with two."

Ty stopped and flexed his free hand. The suitcase in his left felt heavy. He wanted to drop it so he could draw his sidearm and test the lead sniper's boast. Somehow he doubted that she was lying.

Amahle gasped, "She means it, Tyler."

"I bet," he growled. "So when are you handing her over? It needs to be soon. By soon, I mean within the next minute."

The longer they delayed the process, the more risk there was to Amahle. He would *rather* finish the whole thing as soon as possible. By demanding her handover, he was essentially daring She-Wolf to stretch it out longer. Besides, he suspected she had a scheme in mind that involved hitching a ride on the ship post-haste once they made the transfer.

It would be at least a minute before the vessel could moor at the nearest dock.

She-Wolf barked another short, sharp laugh. "Yes, threaten all you want. If my bullet doesn't kill you instantly, you'll be down on your knees and prey for a rifle before you can lay hands on Nikoze. What I don't understand is where all your righteousness comes from.

"Oh, you say, we've no right to harm one who betrayed us all. We've no right to take our payment and move on to greener pastures. I know where that money in your case comes from, my good man. The people who provided it are no better than any of my people, only better at hiding it. If you think you're some knight in shining armor while you do *their* bidding, you're taking the piss out of *yourself.*"

He wondered what she meant by that. Did she have information on the Executives that he didn't?

If he asked her directly, she would only laugh at him. Of that, he felt sure. He opted to try a different tack.

"You won't get very far. You know that, right?" His tone was matter-of-fact, borderline sympathetic as though he regretted having to say it.

"That boat has probably already been noted and logged as an uncleared ship going to and from the island. There will be a blockade. It will pick up you and your followers and send you all to whatever countries you're wanted in. I bet most of you have warrants for your arrest or bounties on your head. Am I right?"

He was half-bluffing. Atlantica didn't have much of a coast guard, let alone a navy, although the Executives were in the process of trying to create one. Furthermore, the American, Canadian, and British Navies tended to watch the waters around the island for suspicious vessels—particularly since the attempted Soviet and Chinese infiltration not long ago.

She-Wolf threw her head back and laughed, her mangy iron-colored hair swaying in the sea breeze. "I'm counting on being caught, you bloody fool. I have a whole trunk full of things from the Coven." Abruptly, her demeanor changed. She grew quieter, more serious. "Toys we took from those two degenerates you were hunting. With those, we go from criminals to valued assets in half a second."

Ty grimaced. She was probably right, and he hadn't thought of that. Behind her, the ship was almost ready to dock, its slick bulk looming closer by the second.

"Most likely it will be the Americans who pick us up," She-Wolf went on. "But suppose it's the Soviets—you're not so naïve as to think they don't have boats and submarines out here, are you?—or, worse yet, the British. Everyone panics. It's tolerable enough for us because then we have a future. And protection from *them*."

Ty peered into her eyes and saw something he hadn't expected. Fear. The hard-edged aging warrior couldn't have been afraid of much, yet she feared the Coven.

His thoughts raced, multiple lines of inquiry straining to come out at the forefront of his mind. Before he could react to the ever-changing situation, She-Wolf tensed and stared at him, growing cold and aggressive again.

"Show me the money. Don't expect to get Nikoze in one piece if you try anything. I *wanted* to kill her, anyway. Half a million American dollars is scarcely enough to change my mind."

Her left hand shot out to clamp around Amahle's throat. Not tightly, but the threat was clear. The woman had no compunction whatsoever about murder. If Ty didn't behave as she wanted him to, she would crush Amahle's windpipe, maybe even break her neck.

Ty exhaled slowly, then lifted the suitcase, held it flat on his left arm, and opened the top with his right. He angled it so the mass of greenbacks within was visible in the lamp's light. Then he selected a bundle of bills at random and flipped through them so She-Wolf could see that they were genuine all the way down. The Execs hadn't attempted to renege.

She-Wolf smiled, and the expression was much like a wild animal lifting its mouth to snarl. "Good. Now, close it and drop it at your feet."

Ty obeyed, clicking the latch shut and letting the case fall in front of him with a *thud*. He was about to insist that She-Wolf keep her end of the bargain and release Amahle. In the back of his mind, he wondered if Daria could see them yet. The dock-yards were a jumbled mess, and in her battered state, it might've taken her too long to clear the many obstacles.

He never got the chance to open his mouth. With a sudden lunge, She-Wolf clubbed Amahle on the back of the head with her pistol butt and yanked the trunk free as she threw her off the dock.

"Goddammit!" Ty exclaimed, eyes bulging as the South African crashed into the water below. He ran and dove off as well, patting himself in midair for his knife. The last thing he saw before he plunged into the sea was She-Wolf snatching up the suitcase and trunk, her face bright with a savage leer of triumph.

CHAPTER EIGHTEEN

The other Ghost-Makers appeared from the surrounding darkness less than three seconds after She-Wolf's hands closed around the suitcase's carrying handle.

Four sprang up seemingly from nowhere around the docks, sequestered under the boardwalk or next to piers while heavily camouflaged. Two more stood on the warehouse roof, unrolled a rope ladder, and clambered down. Another pair rose from dugout pits in the ground before the shoreline where they'd lain covered with blankets strewn with earthen debris. One more emerged from the house closest to the docks.

They were a motley band of men and women, all hard-looking, and all toting rifles except for the man who'd hidden within the house. He had a rocket-propelled grenade launcher, which he kept trained on the idling Autocutioner.

She-Wolf hoisted the suitcase, and in a loud, cawing voice, cried, "Move it! To me. Onto the ship and out. No delays!"

The assassins all jogged toward their leader, hurrying but remaining alert to any further threat from the Executioners. The incoming ship had dropped anchor and was drifting to a halt at the end of Pier Five.

Within the truck, Gage and Dante watched with a growing alarm that bordered on nausea.

"What the *hell?*" Dante blurted. "What happened out there? She did *not* kill Ty. Did she?"

Gage's hands trembled with sick rage, but he forced himself to remain calm. "I do not think so. There was no gunshot. I think —I hope—that she only knocked him off the pier so she could take the money and run."

They could barely see the trade site from where they were parked. They could clearly see the guy who had the RPG pointed at them.

Dante looked at his friend. "Want to hit the gas and see if he misses? Hell, our armor might be good enough to stand up to that thing."

Gage shook his head. "We must not. Even if the blast didn't get to us, the fire might disrupt the Atlanticore engine." It was unnecessary to state what happened to destabilized Atlanticore. They all knew well.

Dante pounded the dashboard with his fist. "Well, as soon as that prick lowers the bazooka, I say we shoot him, at least. They can't kill Ty or Amahle if they're in the water."

Gage clicked off the safety on his AR-10, rolled down the window, and prepared to lean out. "Perhaps." They were up against professional marksmen, and his eyes were not as good as they used to be. Still... he had never been a bad shot, exactly.

In the waters beside Pier Five, Ty swam downward, using broad strokes to cover as wide an area with his hands as he could. Everything was so dark. He knew Amahle had to be right beside him or right beneath him, yet he couldn't see her. The water was cold, and the taste of salt seemed shockingly foul.

Then a hand grabbed his leg. It was more of an accidental flailing than anything intentional. He bobbed toward Amahle, found her arm, and pulled her up while trying to power himself back toward the shore. They weren't far out, and the shallows had to be close enough for them to stand soon.

As he struggled to lift Amahle's head back above the surface, he remembered that her hands were still tied. Gasping and spitting as the water sloshed around him, he pulled out his folding knife and cut her bonds. Then he was able to loop one of her arms over his shoulder.

A moment later, his boots struck mucky ground. He heaved on Amahle, trying to get both of them back to the boardwalk so they could go after the Ghost-Makers.

Amahle hadn't been knocked out cold by the blow, simply stunned and disoriented. Although still not in the best physical or mental shape, she was coming around again, and the way she glanced from side to side suggested that she more or less understood what had happened.

Ty asked, "Can you breathe? Can you talk?"

The South African gasped and spat up a cup's worth of water, then coughed. "Yes. Let me walk."

Ty let her go, and together they scrambled up the beach, slowed by the heavy wetness of their clothes, then remounted the boardwalk in time to see a group of around ten figures hastening along the pier toward the now-immobile ship. A man at the rear of them held an RPG on his shoulder, aimed back at the Auto-cutioner.

"Fuck," he muttered. "If we try anything they'll blow up Dante and Gage."

Amahle shook her head. "They win this game. We have won our lives."

Ty looked at her. She was right, maybe. The thought of simply letting She-Wolf and the others go after their many murderous and double-crossing escapades stung him deeply.

Then, a line of nine people appeared at the ship's rails. Instead of throwing down a ladder, they cocked guns and aimed down.

She-Wolf bellowed, "Scatter!"

Shotguns and rifles *boomed*, and pistols and submachine guns *cracked*. Muzzle flares appeared all along the boat's dock as the Ghost-Makers dropped prone, or dove off the edge into the sea, or sprinted back toward the boardwalk, zigging and zagging. Two of them returned fire, and a man on the ship screamed and toppled off the edge. At practically the same time, one of the Ghost-Makers took a round through the neck or head and dropped like a heavy sack to the pier.

Amahle blurted, "Who are these people?"

Ty helped her duck behind one of the thick pilings that supported the pier. Gunshots rang out all around them. Daria, Gage, and Dante would probably enter the fray too.

"They must be hitmen hired by the Coven," Ty suggested. "Only thing I can think of. We need to stay out of the line of fire, but we also need to get your boss and get both cases back."

Shaking her head to clear it and seeming to draw strength from within herself, Amahle raged, "She is *not* my boss anymore. Get me a gun!"

Ty nodded. "You got it." He drew his 1911, shook out the water, and slowly inhaled through his nose. Things were about to get interesting.

Over in the Autocutioner, Dante was cursing up a storm as he watched absolute chaos erupt. "Goddammit! Who are these fuckers? What the shit is this? Get me over there so I can shotgun their asses!"

Gage had finally decided to lean out the window with his rifle. "Just a moment. Our friend with the rocket appears to be distracted."

He leveled his sights over the man's center of mass. The Ghost-Maker had bolted off the pier once the men on the ship started shooting. Now, having reached cover, he seemed to remember that his specific duty was to stop the Autocutioner from getting involved in the fight. He raised the heavy launcher and looked toward the vehicle.

Gage squeezed the trigger. A single 7.62mm round spiraled straight into the man's lower chest, blasting apart his ribs and bursting his heart like an overripe melon. He fell backward, dropping the RPG launcher as a groaning death rattle escaped his lips.

"All right, Dante." Gage set the rifle beside his seat and gripped the steering wheel. "Now is your chance to ride shotgun." He shifted into drive and slammed on the gas.

Dante bared his teeth in a feral grin and poked his head and shoulders out the window as the Autocutioner shot forward, rumbling along the dirty lanes.

One of the Ghost-Makers, unidentifiable in an all-black outfit and mask, appeared ahead and to the side, trying to hug the wall beside the boardwalk as they slipped away. Seeing the truck bear forth, they raised their rifle.

Dante fired his shotgun faster. The sniper reflexively leapt to the side, dodging the spray of buckshot but bringing themself closer to the truck.

Gage jerked the wheel slightly. The front bumper struck the sniper head-on and pulled them beneath the wheels, causing only the slightest bump in their ride. "Excuse me," Gage said.

Once the buildings fell away beside them and they emerged into the boardwalk area before the docks, Gage braked hard and spun the wheel so the truck swung to a stop with the passenger's-side window facing the ship. People were running everywhere, barking out orders or cries of alarm, and gunshots flew through the night air.

Dante didn't have a clear shot at any of the Ghost-Makers. Since the men on the ship clearly weren't working with the Executioners—and might also be shooting at Ty and Amahle—Dante decided to thin the herd.

Aiming for the railing, he worked the pump and let out three booming blasts at the ship. Men ducked or scattered, and one of them shrieked in pain before toppling against the rail and hanging limply over it, his arms and head dangling.

A second later, the flashes of small explosions appeared beyond the boardwalk wall, creating huge clouds of smoke near the docks that further added to the confusion.

Gage nodded. "Ahh. Daria has found her way here. Good." He raised his rifle again and fired a burst of shots at some men who'd disembarked from the ship to herd the remaining Ghost-Makers into one place.

Two snipers fled back across the boardwalk, slipped around the Autocutioner while Gage and Dante were distracted by the smoke grenades, and into the alley beyond. They ducked low, trying to keep to the shadows that pooled near the edges of the street by the bases of the low buildings. Although fast and stealthy, they were more used to operating in the wilderness. Using manufactured structures for cover wasn't their preferred environment.

They made for a gap in the wooden fence at the rear of the dockyards. Once they were out into the town proper, they could scatter in opposite directions, go to ground, and lose themselves in the Atlantican bush, regrouping with their leader and surviving comrades later.

They didn't get the chance. Daria stepped out from behind a lamppost, Browning Hi-Power in hand, and fired six rounds at their heads and upper bodies before they could bring up their rifles. The first went down instantly with a bullet in his brain and fell into a twisted lump on the street.

The second was able to dodge at first, but Daria's fifth and sixth shots took her in the neck and shoulder. She squawked, blood spraying from her wounds, and collapsed against the alley wall. She tried to bring up her rifle but failed, then rolled on the ground back toward the docks.

Daria lowered her pistol and looked around for any other

threats. Seeing none in her immediate perimeter, she shook her head over the two corpses. "They must not have practiced *close-range* shooting enough," she mumbled.

Then one of the snipers who'd been up on the warehouse roof darted past her. She raised her gun but wasn't fast enough to catch him. The single slug she popped off streaked behind the man and embedded itself in a tree.

As Daria stepped out after him, half a dozen shadowy figures suddenly emerged from the town beyond the fence, surrounding the man before he could evade them in the alleys on the other side of the street. Two held fishing nets mounted on heavy poles, two had crowbars, and two had firearms, a shotgun and a revolver. The Ghost-Maker cursed but raised his hands.

Daria hurried over. "Good job, very responsible of you," she said to the townsfolk. "Hold him there a moment, please. Then we'll take him to the truck, where we have shackles in back. Sir, my employers will want to speak to you."

In a gruff American accent, the man replied, "Great. They'd better protect me from She-Wolf, then."

Back at the juncture of the boardwalk and Pier Five, Ty raised his pistol and emptied an entire magazine, plus the bullet in the chamber, at both groups of their adversaries. The gun boomed five times for the Ghost-Makers, but he couldn't tell if he'd hit any of them.

Then he loaded his spare magazine, raised the weapon, and squeezed off three more shots at the hitmen on the ship. One of them took a round in the spine, given the way he flopped into the water and sank without a struggle. In the wake of the burst of fire, there was a brief lull in the action.

Ty gestured at the pier with his shoulder. "Go!" he told Amahle.

She dashed past him toward the nearest body. It was one of her former compatriots armed with a FAL. She seized the rifle and hopped over to one of the posts, seeking concealment as she looked around for She-Wolf.

"There!" Amahle called. She trained the muzzle on a barely perceptible silhouette moving from one bit of cover to the next on Pier Four, the end of which lay against the stern of the immobile ship. Before she could shoot, the figure vanished.

Ty watched in horror as three men from the ship climbed down onto Pier Five. It looked like one had a coach gun, one a semiautomatic pistol of some sort, and one had a Thompson submachine gun. "We got trouble right here, you know," he called to Amahle.

In response, the guy with the Tommy gun opened fire with a long, chaotic burst that probably emptied at least half of the stick mag. Ty tensed and ducked behind a piling. At least two or three bullets struck the surface behind him, and he was amazed that nothing seemed to hit him. The man must've been blind-firing to cover his friends' advance more than anything.

A rifle *cracked*. Ty peeked around the piling and saw Tommy Gun rolling off the pier with a hole in his face. Glad Amahle was in good fighting form, he returned his attention to the fight, took a bead on the guy with the coach gun, and fired three rounds at him. The man tried to dodge but was too slow, and he groaned and slumped over, the shotgun discharging one of its barrels into the air as he fell.

Suddenly the last man with the pistol aimed at Amahle. Ty saw with horror that she was trying to clear a jam in the rifle. His arm felt like it was moving through molasses as he struggled to bring the 1911 up to finish the man off.

Another thunderous report from a high-powered rifle sounded, and the guy with the pistol toppled over like an overloaded coat rack that someone had tipped. A large portion of his upper head was missing.

Ty's glance flashed to Pier Four, where he could barely make out the silhouette of a lean woman with a rifle vanishing around the ship's stern—presumably making for a ladder, rope, or some other means of scaling and boarding the vessel.

Amahle looked at him. "She-Wolf is getting away!" Before Ty could stop her, she had dashed off the fifth pier, looped around on the main dock, and scudded down the fourth. She paused for about a second, crouching, and Ty saw a small metallic object flash in her hand. Then she waved her free arm at the boat.

She wanted him to board from Pier Five so they could cut off She-Wolf before she could put the ship to sea. A good plan, aside from the fact that he had no idea who or what else might be on the boat or how his friends were doing.

He glanced back and saw Dante and Gage shooting at their foes from the Autocutioner, as well as rising clouds of smoke that had to be Daria's doing. He had little choice but to trust them to fulfill their responsibilities.

"Fine," he grunted and threw himself at the ladder in front of him.

The climb took only seconds but felt longer. As he pulled himself onto the deck, the cabin lay only a short way to his left. When he attempted a tactical reload of his pistol, pocketing the half-empty magazine and replacing it with a full one, a burly shape erupted from the cabin's doorway swinging a sledgehammer.

Ty stepped aside, his eyes widening. He dodged the blow, but the head nicked his pistol and knocked it from his grasp. The man was too slow to bring the heavy weapon back to bear before Ty drew his wakizashi and stabbed him through the side, skewering both lung and heart.

He shouldered Ty off him and seemed about to attempt a last-ditch charge, then collapsed, wheezing. Ty retrieved his 1911 and ran to the ship's stern, jumping onto the sternpost and searching for Amahle and She-Wolf.

The South African was there, crouching and ready, but the Irishwoman was nowhere in sight.

"No!" Amahle scolded him. "Go the other way! She is past us now."

Confirming that she was right, the ship started to move.

CHAPTER NINETEEN

She-Wolf might've known the basics of how to operate a ship, but Ty got a distinct impression that she wasn't an experienced sailor. The vessel bucked and rocked amid the waters *before* the stern clipped the end of the pier.

"Shit!" he cried. The weight of the upper half of his body swayed sideways while his legs tried to stay braced on the stern-post. He ended up tumbling forward past the taffrail to land hard on the rear deck. Once again, his bruised chest assaulted him with pain to protest its maltreatment.

Amahle had remained more or less on her feet, but she'd bent forward and stabilized herself with one hand on the taffrail. The rifle she'd seized dangled precariously from its sling.

The ship's side-to-side rocking subsided as the stern cleared the docks and the vessel chugged toward open water. Ty struggled to his feet, wondering exactly where the crazed riflewoman intended to go. Not only in the sense of where she was trying to sail to but also where on this ship she planned to sequester herself.

Ty's pistol was out in his hands. He kept it in a low ready position, uncertain if any crewmen remained on the ship. If so, were they part of the same hit squad that had opened fire on the Ghost-Makers, or were they innocent workers roped into doing the menial labor that would ferry the hitmen to their destination?

Ty looked up at Amahle. She'd crawled down from the taffrail and was trying to get his attention. She unslung her rifle and gestured with her chin and eyes at herself, then at the starboard or far side of the cabin.

She wanted to flank her former boss. Ty nodded and moved across the elevated rear portion of the deck, toward the open door where the ship's controls lay.

A flit of motion, barely noticeable, appeared before him combined with the ever so faint reflection of the ship's lights off a curved surface of blued steel. Through instinct rather than conscious thought, Ty threw himself to the side, behind the cabin's corner, in time to avoid the bullet that exploded from She-Wolf's rifle.

He raised his pistol and blind-fired one shot around the corner. Feet moved across the deck, and by the time he'd poked his head around, a lithe shadow had vanished into the jumble of equipment beyond the cabin near the ship's center.

Another shot rang out as Amahle fired at She-Wolf. Ty doubted she could see anything. It was likely a probing shot. The older, more experienced woman would've realized that and been unfazed by it. It was practically a formality.

Ty clenched his teeth. That there were two of them and only one of their adversary was their sole advantage. She-Wolf might well be their superior in every other respect.

Still, she couldn't hide forever. The ship was only so long. She would be unable to flee far.

Ty called to Amahle, "Watch for her down there. I'm going to check the cabin."

The South African nodded. She climbed atop the cabin and crouched there, her rifle held ready. He noticed that to give herself a better field of view, she wasn't using the scope but simply looking over it and more or less point-shooting.

He inhaled and swung himself around to the cabin's doorway, his pistol ready.

Within were four men, looking frightened and confused. "She made us turn around," one of them stammered. A bead of sweat worked its way down the side of his face. "Those other men with the guns were the ones who wanted us to dock here. Nobody told us nothing. We're not part of any of this. We just sail the ship!"

Ty stared the man down and examined the others. He stayed on the threshold, where he would have somewhat better cover and concealment in case She-Wolf reemerged and went on the offensive. There wasn't time to deal with everyone at once.

"Okay," he said, "I believe you, and I don't want to hurt you. But if any of you try to shoot me in the back, you'd better not miss."

With that, he stepped away from the cabin laterally, holding his 1911 toward the prow, where his enemy had fled.

Nothing, so far. He looked up at Amahle again. "Don't shoot through the lower hull of the ship. Sinking is the last thing we need to happen right now."

Amahle gave him a sharp squint of annoyance. Then from somewhere below and in front of them, a rough-edged, Irish-accented voice cackled. "She's not that stupid. I trained her far better than that! You seem to have a knack for underestimating people, Executioner."

Ty's head moved in short jerks as he tried to follow the sounds. It was as though She-Wolf were moving around in erratic waves as she spoke, yet he could neither hear her feet nor see her shadow.

Amahle said, "She's throwing her voice. It's a skill we all learned. She speaks in many directions to disguise her position."

She-Wolf overheard and laughed, and the harsh mockery of it leaping around the ship's deck was downright unnerving.

Ty advanced two paces. Between a hatch leading below deck and two large masses of cargo, he figured the Irishwoman was hiding in one of three likely locations. "Okay, where is she, then?"

"How would I know?" Amahle protested.

Something jumped up from behind a crate. Ty reflexively covered it with his muzzle and fired once. It didn't react to the shot but flopped through the air to land on the deck and essentially turned into a puddle. It was an empty coat.

Then another rifle shot rang out from behind a crate at least five yards from where the coat had appeared. Amahle threw herself off the cabin and rolled against the starboard rail, gasping in pain.

Ty ran toward her, knowing he was exposing himself to fire but too worried to care. "Are you hit?"

She waved toward the lower deck. "No. Watch her! She is trying to get a better position on us. Or lure us into a trap."

As Ty's brain raced with plans and tactics for flushing the woman out, one of the men in the cabin leaned out and said, "We got a transmission from the Brits. They say if we go much farther, they'll have to scoop us up. We think the goddamn Russians might be out there, too."

Ty cursed under his breath. Their time was limited. If they reached the naval blockade, She-Wolf would get away with all she'd done, settling into protective custody as a witness and informant, selling tales of the dirty dealings on Atlantica to whichever government acquired her first.

He made eye contact with Amahle again, and she nodded.

Together, in tandem, they advanced, employing no fancy tricks, only a steady, thorough patrol, relying upon the fact that both of them were well-honed shooters with fast reflexes. Still, She-Wolf's speed, even at her somewhat advanced age, was terrifying. Ty had no certainty that the two of them could overcome her, should it all come down to a duel of trigger fingers.

Amahle covered him with her rifle while he went to the hatch. He was putting himself at risk, but he didn't have time to do everything safely. He flipped it open with his foot and covered the space beyond with his gun's muzzle, ready to shoot at anything that moved.

There was nothing so far. A single electric lamp shone from somewhere below. He looked up again to ensure that She-Wolf wasn't in sight, then descended the sharply angled stepladder while holding the 1911 in his right hand and guiding himself with his left.

Below deck was nothing more than a jumble of garbage and low-quality wares, most of them covered with rotting canvas. If the Irishwoman had snuck down here, she might easily be able to hide until they reached the blockade.

As soon as the deck moved beyond Ty's head, a shot thundered above him. Amahle's body hit the surface and rolled, and his heart jumped into his throat as he pulled himself back up.

"No!" Amahle screamed.

Ty ducked his head back down and felt a bullet whiz through his hair, parting it mere inches above his left eye. Then Amahle returned fire, sending two shots toward the prow.

Ty climbed through the hatch, closed it, and stabilized himself in a shooting position. "Well." He sighed. "At least we know she's still out in the invigorating sea air." Beyond that, though, he had no idea where she'd fled to.

Amahle, however, had rushed to the ship's port side, opposite his starboard position. With a certain amount of concern, he watched as she slung the rifle over her shoulder and crawled on the outside of the railing. Between her dark skin and dark clothes, it would make her hard to see against the night sky. He wondered how long she could take the strain.

She-Wolf's voice answered his thoughts. "You're both

wounded and tired. Why are you wasting your time and energy? You'll be lucky if the English send you home instead of arresting you. The Soviets will put a bullet in the back of your necks."

Ty had to admit that for someone he hadn't known long, he was getting tired of listening to her.

"Bullshit," he growled. "This whole scheme of yours was a long shot to begin with. Now the odds have shifted against you even more. You're desperate, and you're in denial about it. You think we didn't have a backup plan of our own? Anything you say is nothing more than an empty bluff at this point. Just give up."

When She-Wolf responded, she threw her voice again, obscuring its exact origin. "Oh, and you think I lived this long by giving up every time a railroad worker like you or a stupid girl like Nikoze tries to scare me with big talk?"

Yet she was running out of real estate. The prow of a single ship was only so big. She might be able to evade them for a few more minutes to make it harder for them to target her position, but the game would be up soon.

Ty decided to inform her of the fact. He'd always heard that cornered wolves were dangerous. They fought with a level of ferociousness that few humans could comprehend. Ty liked to think he was one of the people who *did* understand such things. There was enough of a rational human being in her—a calculating, self-interested human being, that was—that she might decide that turning herself in was the better option in the absence of any other real choice.

"You don't have any place left to hide," he shouted. "You can't take us both on at once. You're good, but not *that* good. Don't be an idiot and fight to the death. Surrender, and maybe we can come to an arrangement."

The aging woman laughed, the harshness of the sound seeming to mingle with the rush of the waves. "Oh! An *arrangement*. So says the man known as the Executioner. Everyone knows your reputation. You're as much a killer by nature as I am, maybe more. Your arrangement will give me one last meal before you slice my head off with your bent sword, won't it? Come out, then, and try it right now."

Ty grimaced. She had a point. Atlantica's largely unwritten code of justice would probably condemn her to death for her many crimes and betrayals. If the Executives got hold of her, the Coven might well pull out all the stops to silence her before she could talk too much, anyway.

In a way, Ty almost pitied her. She had no chance...unless she could kill him and Amahle. If so, she could take the ship out to the east until the British Navy or the Russians picked her up.

As if reading his mind, she added, "It will be fun, truth be told. I'm a more wanted woman in England than anywhere else, but even those bastards would make me a better deal than you could. Knowing what I can bring them. Maybe if you'll stop acting a fool, I'll tell them to turn you loose back to Atlantica and be done with it."

He doubted that. She'd gone back on her word enough times as it was. With him, and with Amahle, too.

Ty glanced up at his new partner. Amahle was still creeping along the outside of the port-side railing. How she managed such a strenuous ordeal after all she'd been through—beaten half to death and nearly drowned, among everything else—he had only the vaguest idea. She was made of truly stern stuff.

Their eyes met. Ty held up a finger, hoping she understood that he was signaling her to wait and follow his lead. Then he picked up a barrel that had nothing to speak of in it and hurled it over the edge.

"Amahle!" he cried, trying to sound as emotional as possible. "*No!*" The barrel struck the water with a noticeable crash before slipping beneath the waves and being lost in the ship's churning wake.

Then a dark shape flitted somewhere ahead of him, behind a double stack of heavy crates, and the echoing report of two rifle rounds rang out. Ty's jaw dropped. She-Wolf had fired one shot each at the port and starboard rails, narrowly missing Amahle. She couldn't see her former protege. However, she'd somehow known or suspected that Ty was trying to pull a ruse on her.

She'd taken a chance in moving and shooting. Ty had narrowed down her position to only about two spots. He *might* be able to storm back there and get the jump on her. It was a question of who would be faster to fire.

Ty had outdrawn several men with his pistol holstered. Right now, he held it in his hand. The advantage might well be his. Still, roiling away deep in his gut was a primal fear, the anxiety that he would prove not good enough when it counted most. She-Wolf handled her rifle like it was part of her body.

He shouted, "I saw that you know. You can't hide any longer. We'll—"

In the same split second it took him to realize he'd made an idiotic mistake in using the word *we*, the dark shape appeared again behind a different stack of crates and fired.

Ty squeezed off a round from his 1911. It struck the edge of the crate while the shape vanished, and the rifle bullet whizzed past his ear. Then She-Wolf's gun cracked again.

"Oh, my God," Ty groaned. He spun and flung himself to the left. She-Wolf had barely tried to hit him. She was only distracting him while she went for Amahle, having guessed that her ex-employee was crawling somewhere along the port side of the ship.

The first thing he saw was Amahle, her mouth opening and closing with wordless anguish and fear as she tumbled from the railing, caught a rope strung along the side of the ship to hold the life preservers, and tried to pull herself back up. She had no leverage, and the boat's increasingly bumpy motion and growing salty winds didn't make it any easier.

Either she would hold on as long as she could, or Ty would pull her up. Otherwise, she was dead.

The second thing Ty saw, and his gun hand came up almost before his conscious mind was aware of it, was She-Wolf taking a bead on him. He squeezed off a shot from his pistol.

Once more, he hit nothing, and the dark shape disappeared behind the cargo.

There was no time to think. Ty plunged around the other side of the crates, pistol held at eye level in both hands, ready to shoot the instant that—

Then he froze. She-Wolf was there, kneeling next to the prow ladder that descended from the deck, with her rifle braced atop another empty barrel. He could tell at once that she *knew* he was there and was perfectly well aware that he'd gotten the drop on her. Her eyes were focused elsewhere.

Her voice was soft when the grizzled woman spoke, yet Ty heard every word clearly. "Do you think you can send me to the next world with that thing before I can send *her* along ahead of me?"

Ty swallowed. He kept one eye on She-Wolf, but with the other tried to glance at Amahle. He could barely see her from here, only a dark shape thrashing pitifully against the elements as she struggled to hold on to the rope, which was sinking lower as it gradually came loose from the side of the ship. It looked like she was reaching into her clothes for something. He prayed that it wasn't a knife, that she wasn't about to cut herself loose and take her chances with the sea simply for his sake.

He proclaimed, "Horseshit. I don't care how good you are. You can't hit her under these conditions, especially missing your good eye. You missed me a second ago. You're not the dead shot you're reputed to be, are you?"

Amahle's only chance was that She-Wolf would change her mind and try to kill him first. At least that would be a fair fight. It would be nearly impossible for She-Wolf to pivot her rifle before Ty could put a .45 round in her. There was still a chance that he might only get a glancing hit on her skull while she was still able to shoot him before she expired. Then Amahle would sink into the ocean with no one to pull her up.

She-Wolf sneered, "I've got her face right in my sights. It looks like she might be crying. I expected better of her. And she's got a knife! About to end it all. Seems pointless."

With a speed that shocked him, She-Wolf somehow half-kicked, half-threw the barrel under her rifle at him before he could react. The curved wooden surface struck his gun, knocking it and his arms aside while one of his feet slipped and he fell to one knee. His eyes bulged as he saw the Irishwoman leveraging the muzzle of her gun directly at his forehead.

But when the gunshot came, it was far too quiet. Too weak and far away.

Ty blinked. The rifle was drooping from She-Wolf's grasp, its muzzle dragging against the deck as the tall woman staggered back two steps, her face drawn with pain and horror. Light from the cabin reflected off a wave, and Ty saw a tiny red hole in She-Wolf's right shoulder blade, blossoming to a larger exit wound through her lung.

Amahle hadn't pulled a knife. She'd pulled out She-Wolf's .32 revolver, which the older woman must've dropped when she leapt from the pier onto the ship. Amahle must have recovered it. A weapon designed to be fired accurately from across a card table or less adeptly from across a single room. Amahle had fired it while dangling from a rope in the wind at least fifty yards away.

She-Wolf opened her mouth as though to scream or curse, but only a hollow, rasping gurgle came out. She dropped her rifle altogether, letting it clatter against the deck, then sagged onto the ladder behind her. For a second, her features contorted in savage hatred. Then she relaxed, looking nearly peaceful as she let go, plummeted overboard, and vanished into the sea.

Ty stared at the now-empty spot where a second ago, the woman had stood. His brain didn't immediately grasp that

Amahle was shouting at someone else. Out of the corner of his eye, he saw one of the crew members descending from the bridge and pulling up the half-loosened rope.

A minute later, the ship began to turn, swinging a wide arc through the waves before heading back toward the island.

Amahle came up to him. Ty was still blinking at the ladder.

"What are you doing?" she asked.

He looked up, half-startled. "Sorry. I should have, uh, helped you, but it looks like that guy had it under control."

She stared at him bug-eyed, which seemed odd to him. If anything, he should be the one wearing that expression after witnessing the single finest piece of pistol marksmanship he'd ever seen or perhaps even heard of.

He coughed. "I'm glad you're okay, though. I had an idea."

CHAPTER TWENTY

Ned Wandrei, at the age of sixty-eight, was more or less considered the leader of the village now. Officially, a whole council of elders and respected citizens ran the community. He was the eldest one who was still in good health and of sound mind. When he spoke, people listened. He'd never thought of himself as a leader, but such was the way things had played out.

Now, he was here at the eastern dockyards along with nine other people from the farming valley, selected as representatives to finally finish their business from three days ago. The event still left a sour, almost sickening taste in his mouth.

What was supposed to be a simple handover of the hated Ashcroft twins had become a chaotic melee. What was supposed to bring closure and peace had only made the whole village that much more frightened and sorrowful.

Neither Ned Wandrei nor anyone else had wanted to go. The Executioners had a pretty good reputation in most of Atlantica, but the way they'd botched things three mornings ago made the community seriously doubt their trustworthiness.

Still, they claimed to have wrapped things up and captured the people who were truly responsible for all the horror.

So, the ten elders had made the journey to the eastern coast. They waited on the boardwalk next to Pier Five, watching the afternoon sun peeking through the drifting clouds to scatter golden light across the waves before hiding behind them again and blanketing the scene in dimmer, softer hues.

At last, a ship approached. It wasn't all that big; a cargo hauler operated by a small independent contractor, probably. It went straight to the pier. To either side of the ten elders, the dockworkers who inhabited the adjacent town loaded and unloaded a commercial barge or repaired a couple of boats.

When the ship stopped, a motley crew of people appeared at the railing. Foremost among the group were the Executioners. There were five of them now, the four who'd shown up in the valley the other day and a relatively young black woman with old scars on her face and heavy bandages over various parts of her body. She was perhaps the most somber of the group, but none were exactly cheerful.

With them were two men in dark clothes and chain fetters with black hoods over their heads, obviously prisoners of the Executioners. Those two carried a pair of clearly occupied body bags.

Ned gave them a hard look as Tyler Katakura stepped forward and announced, "Please board the ship. No one will harm you. You may bring your weapons in the understanding that they're only for your peace of mind. We're here today to see justice concluded, not to pursue schemes or petty acts of revenge."

Mutters went around the group. Ned turned to eye them. "We agreed to settle this and to be reasonable about it. Let's go. If they betray us, well, everyone will hear about it. We got these witnesses all over the docks." He gestured at the workers to either side of them. "No one would trust the Executioners ever again."

Ty nodded, clearly understanding the implied threat.

The ten elders boarded the ship with Ty and Dr. Dante Costa

helping them. Once everyone stood on the deck, the ship pushed out to sea, not far enough for the dockyards to become invisible, but to the point where the only thing nearby was the choppy blue surface of the Atlantic, the coastline having dwindled to relative insignificance.

Far enough out that anything dropped overboard would be unlikely to wash ashore.

Ned breathed in. "All right, let's talk it over, then." He put his thick, calloused hands in his pockets and waited.

Ty nodded and drew himself up to his full height, looking over the elders with a calm expression and one hand resting against the hilt of the sword by his side. "What we do here today is intended as an olive branch we extend to your community, but also as a new method of dealing with the guilty. Our mission to bring justice to this island hasn't always been easy, but we've done our best. We regret the events of three days past and would prefer that such a thing never happens again."

The elders grumbled their begrudging agreement.

Ty went on. "You're here to bear witness to the fact that we've discharged the duty of *judgment* to Atlantica itself. We're delegating some of our authority to the people whom we serve."

Ned queried, "So where are them two you brought the other day? The last ones who were hunting our people down like dogs. Didn't let them get away, did you?" The two hooded prisoners didn't appear to be siblings. They were too big, and both looked male.

Daria Barruk and Dr. Gaje Gurung took the body bags from the prisoners and unzipped them, exposing the faces of the corpses within. Ty waved at them. "Look."

Ned moved a couple of steps nearer, trying not to let his hesitancy be too obvious. He didn't particularly want to get closer to the Executioners, nor did he want to examine human corpses in detail or get a face full of the accompanying smell. But, he had his duties. He looked.

The one on the left was undoubtedly Tilda Ashcroft. Though somewhat distorted by death, her pale skin, dark hair, and mocking twist of the lips were still easily recognizable. The one on the right was harder to identify. It was probably her brother, but the face had been damaged and was horrible to see.

Ty explained, "It's Hugh Ashcroft. He died of a gunshot to the throat, then a blast buried him under a bunch of debris in a crater out in the jungle. We had to dig him out. If you feel like prying the eyelids open, you'll see that he has the same eyes as his sister.

"Speaking of which, Tilda fell out of a helicopter and got herself skewered on a tree. Neither of them escaped. They've ended up in the same place as those they victimized."

Ned grimaced. "I'll take your word for it." Turning to the other community leaders, he said, "It's them. The Ashcrofts. They're dead, then."

The other nine elders filed past the two bags, glancing briefly at the faces of the deceased and shuddering. It was an ugly sight, but knowing that those who'd tormented them had paid the price at least made them feel that the horror was finally over.

Then Ty and Dante brought out a pair of heavy concrete blocks, tying them to the body bags with steel chains, and the four Executioners dumped the corpses over the side of the ship while the farmers watched. The blocks went first, sinking beneath the waves and dragging the body bags down with them before vanishing into the Atlantic.

As everyone stepped back from the railing, Ned gestured at the two anonymous prisoners. "These men. Who are they and why are they here, if we may ask?"

Ty glanced sidelong at them before turning his eyes back to the community leaders. "They're the last of the Ghost-Makers in Atlantica. A mercenary sniper group, assassins for hire. They were the ones who opened fire on everyone in the valley three days ago when we were first trying to hand over Hugh and Tilda.

"We killed their leader and most of the rest of them in a battle that took place at that very dockyard two nights ago." He pointed back at the shore. "We captured one of them as he was fleeing, and the other was picked up by the British Navy while trying to escape the island in a stolen boat. They handed him back over to us."

A woman among the elders said, "Oh, likely story. Maybe it's true. It was all hidden sharpshooters, it was. Could well be people like that. But who were they hired to kill?"

Ty cleared his throat. "Us, as well as the Ashcrofts. We're looking into who hired them. But it's over, now. The lives of these two belong to you."

Ned frowned. He hadn't expected a wrinkle of this nature. "I say we take them back to face the community and see what everyone says." Looking over his shoulder, it looked like most of the others were willing to agree with his suggestion.

Ty held up a hand and shook his head. "No. You are the community. Its representatives. Either they die now and go into the water, or you renounce your claim upon them."

Ned turned away from the Executioners and huddled with the others. There was no space for true privacy, but they spoke among themselves in low voices. It took three or four minutes for them to decide what to do. When they broke the huddle, Ned spoke for them all.

"If what you say is true," he declared, "let them be punished now and be done with it. We'll accept the burden on the condition of your honesty. Take off the hoods first, so we at least remember them as men."

Ty gave a slow bow of the head. "We haven't lied to you about who they are. Your conditions are acceptable."

He pulled off the coverings, exposing both men's faces to the crowd. One was a beefy white man who looked angry and defiant, the other a slightly built black man who tried to maintain his dignity although a tear had rolled down his cheek. The second one opened his mouth, about to say something, to plead his case.

From behind the pair, Daria stepped forth, Browning pistol in her hand, and waved for the farmers to stand aside. They did in a hurry. She put a round into the back of each man's head, the pistol barking and falling silent as the Ghost-Makers slumped to the deck, instantly dead.

The newest member of the Executioners was the only one who hadn't participated in anything thus far, and she continued to stand apart from the others, watching with rather sad eyes as Gage and Dante handled the two new corpses. As with the siblings, they weighted the bodies with chained blocks and tossed them overboard to be claimed by the ocean.

Through it all, Amahle Nikoze, the order's newest member, had tears swelling in her eyes. Closing them, she hummed a soft song with long notes filled with deep emotion. Although beautiful in a way, it sounded exactly like what it was—a funeral dirge.

One of the community leaders, an ex-pastor named Simon, protested, "Did we really have to do that? Did we have to *see* that? They could have been banished or put in jail. Was it right to—"

"Stop." Tyler cut him off. "Your people executed judgment, and we served justice." With hard eyes, he looked into the faces of each of the ten representatives. "Yes... Men and women still died, and it's right to mourn that."

With their dark business concluded, the Executioners directed the crew to take the ship back to the docks. It turned and anchored again at the empty pier, where they let Ned Wandrei and the others off. The ten walked slowly across the boardwalk and vanished into the town before they rejoined their chauffeurs to begin the journey back to their valley, which would hopefully return to peace.

Ty, Daria, Gage, Dante, and Amahle remained on board. The ship pulled away from the docks once more and headed southwest. It would stop next at the main harbor of Atlantica Metro, from whence the five would make their way back to their headquarters in the city.

Ty hadn't missed Amahle's soft weeping. He wandered over and put a hand on her shoulder, using a gentle but deliberate motion so he didn't startle her. "How are you doing, Am? You okay?"

Her shoulders hunched for a second, then relaxed. "My tears were for many things. In part, they were for those last two men, the last of the Ghost-Makers in Atlantica. If anyone else remains in another country, they'll become independent, and I'll never see them again. I knew those two men. I fought with them, laughed and cried with them at times. I saved one's life in Africa. I also shed tears for my previous life."

Ty waited and listened as she swallowed and wiped her eyes and nose.

"There are many things to which I had to... resign myself, I believe is the expression. I had to forgive myself. When working with those people, I did necessary and terrible things. They weren't always so pure or simple as I had thought. I am trying, now, to make peace with what I've done. There is nothing I can do about the past. It must be left as it is; we cannot change it."

Ty moved his hand down from his shoulder to her hand and clasped it. His voice was soft. "You can try to live today better than you did yesterday."

"Yes." Amahle didn't object to his gesture and gripped his hand tighter. "I suppose that is all any of us can do." She looked down at their hands, then up at the horizon, where the sun would soon set beyond the water's rim and close the door on another day.

CHAPTER TWENTY-ONE

It had been about three weeks since the burials at sea, which they'd all come to think of as Amahle's first day as an Executioner. In the intervening period, they'd been busy. Today was the first day they'd had to lounge around the lab with drinks, sharing stories of their recent exploits.

"So," Dante railed, finishing the story he'd begun telling five or ten minutes ago and gesturing with a half-drained bottle of beer. "It turns out they were trying to use *rubbing alcohol*. They thought that if you watered it down and added some fucking corn syrup, it would make a perfectly good replacement and no one would notice."

He broke off laughing, then his guffaws trailed away, and he stared into the mouth of his bottle. "Too bad about what happened to those people, though. Shit. I guess we have to cope with the ugly side of the job somehow. I heard cops say stuff like that back in the States. They laughed because if they didn't, they'd cry."

Ty managed a dry, sardonic chuckle. He'd heard about the whole situation. People were dropping dead or got hauled off to the hospital's poison ward. Since Dante was a physician, they'd assigned him to investigate. He'd traced the problem back to a group of moonshiners who seemed perplexed about why the Executioners were investigating them since Atlantica had no specific laws about distilleries, drug consumption, or anything of the sort.

Daria and Amahle also smiled and shook their heads at the sheer stupidity. They'd seen similar things recently—incidents of no intentional evil, only a degree of carelessness and thoughtlessness that became lethal at times.

The only one not participating in the conversation was Gage. He was nearby, listening but not talking—he was busy, after all.

The room that had become known as the lab was originally a study or large office on the second floor. Once everyone agreed that Gage could take things apart and tinker with strange or dangerous materials indoors, they stipulated that it should be on the opposite side of the building from their sleeping quarters and as far as possible from the infirmary.

There were three tables set up along the walls and on the room's far side. The other four Executioners sat in a ring of chairs on the side closer to the door. At present, Gage was poking through the various items they'd recovered from the Ashcrofts' trunk.

He'd spread the trunk's contents out on the tables and had spent the last week or more cataloging them, performing minor tests, and in some cases, disassembling items to determine what they were and what their purpose might be.

Most of the gadgets that Hugh and Tilda had tried to escape with were unidentifiable. They might as well have been artifacts from a different planet, at first glance. After examining them in more detail, Gage was slowly gaining a better understanding of what they were dealing with. The study of ancient Atlantican devices had been his archaeology specialty here before he'd joined the Executioners.

All the devices contained either Atlanticore crystals—as

expected—or entire preexisting artifacts, which were usually powered by Atlanticore and integrated into the Coven's new inventions. He'd tried dating the materials and checking for sediments that were traceable to particular periods. However, the Coven had cleaned everything well before assembly, not to mention the specimens were contaminated with newer debris from the helicopter crash and the battle at the dockyards.

Ty glanced at the Nepali. "Hey, Gage. What's the latest news on all that stuff?"

Everyone else turned their head toward him, as well. They were all curious.

Gage had kind of been hoping they would ask. "Well, the modern components all seem to be rather common materials—things they could've purchased from multiple suppliers and sources. They seem to have tried that since none of the pieces or fittings share a single source. Whoever is doing this wants to make it as difficult as possible for us to pinpoint who they are or from where they operate."

"Hah," Daria scoffed. "I expected as much. This Coven has been nothing but secretive since we've heard of them. Did I mention that even those mercenaries on the ship had no idea who they were working for? The ones who tried to silence the Ghost-Makers before we could intercept them. The other day I finally tracked down their contact. He was some middle-grade fixer type. He thought he was picking up a nice commission for a simple job and knew virtually nothing about whom he was setting things up for. Hardly anyone has even *heard* of the Coven of Miracles."

Ty clenched his hands, suddenly impatient. They'd been trying to gain dirt on the Coven for months now, pursuing it almost obsessively in between their more banal duties. Recovering the trunk had been a major breakthrough. Yet it hadn't truly told them much of use.

"Yeah, yeah," he rumbled. "That's what we figured. This is

mostly all a rehash of what we already know. Gage, you were the one who said we needed to take a break to hear what you had to say. What's the big revelation? The rest of us have active cases to get back to."

Gage seemed wholly untroubled by Ty's crabbiness. He retained his usual sanguine demeanor. "Do not worry. I am getting to the point. Yes, the Coven could get the mundane materials from various sources, but they couldn't pluck the ancient artifacts from haphazard places with any degree of ease. They also failed to scrub down their findings as well as they thought."

Dante, the only other Executioner with advanced education, perked up. "So, the sediment dating finally turned up something? Hoo boy. That's big, if so."

Gage picked up one of the items, which looked faintly like the planet Saturn. A hollow sphere of shiny metal contained a crystal with a ring around its circumference.

"I was able to take small samples of the corrosion that was still present. Then I cross-referenced this with the results of the soil and geological surveys that are constantly being done and updated. One most excellent thing about Atlantica is that they're keeping scientific records as more of the island is dug up for plunder and development."

"Oooh." Dante drained his beer and leaned forward. The others were also alert, even if they knew less about the minutiae of science than the New Yorker and the Nepali did.

Gage's face dropped into a slight scowl. "At first, the findings were sufficiently bizarre that I thought someone had made an error and that I'd wasted my time. There was a concerning, almost staggering amount of variety in the samples. It was as though an excavation taking place in, let us say, Kansas turned up samples that should be from Brazil, Alaska, China, and Australia. In this case, it all seems to come from different regions of Atlantica."

"Okay, what the hell does that mean?" Ty replied.

Amahle looked at him with slight disapproval. "Be patient, Tyler." She was the boldest when it came to chiding the dreaded Katakura. It made the others wonder what had transpired between the two during their flight through the jungle and their duel with She-Wolf on the ship.

Gage held up a single finger. "I had to change my approach. Once I stopped looking to see if they all came from the same dig sites, things became clearer. I examined only the properties themselves, which were associated with the geological data that matched the corrosion samples. It occurred to me to look at who laid claim to those lands. Then I found a pattern."

Daria arched her eyebrows. "This ought to be illuminating."

The Gurkha's eyes went distant, and it was as though a dark cloud had drifted over his head. "All the corrosion markers connect to land owned by the blind trust under which the Executives operate and manage their holdings."

He paused as uncomfortable silence expanded to fill the whole room.

"So," Gage concluded, "either the Coven of Miracles is stealing these prizes out from under the Executives' watch—"

Ty interrupted him with a sudden growl. "*Or* the very people picking up our tab are also collecting artifacts for some kind of doomsday scheme."

He thought back to Lucas Montrosse, the Executive who'd originally hired him and acted as Eleanor's handler. Ty had personally cut off his head after he found that Lucas was manipulating them all as part of a plot to exploit the land for Atlanticore and kill off the workers who might be able to bear witness against him.

Aside from Lucas, he hadn't met any of the others. Eleanor handled everything on their behalf.

Ty looked askance at Amahle's scarred face, drawn with vulnerability and pain, and added. "Who knows how often we've been used to help them?"

Dante leaned back in his chair with a deep frown marring his handsome features. "Yeah," he muttered. "I think we all need another drink."

THE STORY CONTINUES

The story continues with book five, *Justice is Not Blind*, available now at Amazon.

Claim your copy today!

AUTHOR NOTES MICHAEL ANDERLE

JANUARY 6, 2021

Thank you for not only reading this series but these author notes here in the back as well.

I have been thinking a lot about a bunch of acronyms and stuff such as NFT, Partial NFT,

DeFi, Blockchain, bitcoin, and ICO, which all revolve around one concept.

What is money?

Obviously, it is a figment of our imagination. We use it to grease the skids of exchanging work and wealth with one another, sometimes globally with people we don't know and possibly can't trust.

It shouldn't work.

Think about it like this. If I were to come up to you and offer you a cotton-based paper product in exchange for something of yours worth $80.00, would you take it?

Unlikely.

However, put some green ink and hard to duplicate stuff in it, and now that cotton-based paper is worth $100.00 US and you would exchange something very tangible for something…kinda worthless, but we BELIEVE it is worth $100.00

I am heading out to CES (Consumer Electronics Show) in a few minutes to check on some NFT (Non-Fungible Tokens) and DeFi (Decentralized Finance) products because I've believed since writing my first series (*The Kurtherian Gambit*) in 2015, "Follow the money."

People have been pouring ludicrous amounts of money into DeFi and ICOs (Initial Coin Offering) with Blockchain integration for a few years, and I'm curious about it. I don't have any investments in the area, but what if I build something I *do* know a lot about (publishing) and have a thousand people join me on the trip?

It might be a blast.

I can't do it in the stock market I don't think, but I might be able to with the new stuff. Mind you, it's not easy. The US Government already calls ICOs an investment vehicle and has put all sorts of regulations around it, so it's not the Wild West anymore.

Unfortunately, I'm still ignorant on the subject, even AFTER reading about it. Thus, my second day of going to CES.

I am working on ways we could ramp production back to 400 books a year. To accomplish that goal, I suspect I'll need to figure out new ways to finance it. I have many efforts running right now on the marketing side to kick it into gear. With that many books, the marketing effort has to be monstrous in scale.

The reason I bring this up is, I see all of these disruptive technologies as being a bit like the heart of Atlantica—something new in the world that will forever change the ways we as a society move forward.

It's Matrix-like in my mind.

So, I'm off to CES and look forward to chatting with you in the next book!

Ad Aeternitatem,
Michael Anderle

OTHER ATLANTICA BOOKS

John Chambers Books

Her Mother's Pendant (Book 1)

The Mystery Deepens (Book 2)

One Last Choice (Book 3)

Valentina Winters

The Red Countess (Book 1)

One Night to Kill (Book 2)

One Death Too Few (Book 3)

Terra Kris

She is the Law (Book 1)

Law or Justice (Book 2)

Justice Served (Book 3)

Santana Sokolov

Law of the Jungle (Book 1)

Inner City Jungle (Book 2)

Rumble in the Jungle (Book 3)

BOOKS BY MICHAEL ANDERLE

Sign up for the LMBPN email list to be notified of new releases and special deals!

http://lmbpn.com/email

For a complete list of books by Michael Anderle, please visit:

www.lmbpn.com/ma-books/

CONNECT WITH THE AUTHOR

Connect with Michael Anderle

Website: http://lmbpn.com

Email List: http://lmbpn.com/email/

https://www.facebook.com/LMBPNPublishing

https://twitter.com/MichaelAnderle

https://www.instagram.com/lmbpn_publishing/

https://www.bookbub.com/authors/michael-anderle